Ruthless Hearts 3

**Lock Down Publications and Ca$h
Presents**
Ruthless Hearts 3
A Novel by *Willie Slaughter*

Lock Down Publications
P.O. Box 944
Stockbridge, Ga 30281

Visit our website @
www.lockdownpublications.com

Copyright 2020 Willie Slaughter
Ruthless Hearts 3

Lock Down Publications
Like our page on Facebook: Lock Down Publications @
www.facebook.com/lockdownpublications.ldp
Cover design and layout by: **Dynasty Cover Me**
Book interior design by: **Shawn Walker**
Edited by: **Lashonda Johnson**

Stay Connected with Us!

Text **LOCKDOWN** to 22828 to stay up-to-date with new releases, sneak peaks, contests and more…

Thank you.

Submission Guideline.

Submit the first three chapters of your completed manuscript to ldpsubmissions@gmail.com, subject line: Your book's title. The manuscript must be in a .doc file and sent as an attachment. Document should be in Times New Roman, double spaced and in size 12 font. Also, provide your synopsis and full contact information. If sending multiple submissions, they must each be in a separate email.

Have a story but no way to send it electronically? You can still submit to LDP/Ca$h Presents. Send in the first three chapters, written or typed, of your completed manuscript to:

LDP: Submissions Dept
P.O. Box 944
Stockbridge, Ga 30281

DO NOT send original manuscript. Must be a duplicate.

Provide your synopsis and a cover letter containing your full contact information.

Thanks for considering LDP and Ca$h Presents.

Willie Slaughter

Prologue

The main piece of the body laid on the asphalt on its back next to the dumpster in the alleyway. In the predawn gloom, everything looked grey, but there were splashes of blood around the body. Jennifer, Director Wade Stevens, and three other federal agents looked at the horrific scene. While they took in the sight of the limbless corpse Jennifer decided it was the perfect time to implement her plan.

"Director Stevens," she began as she turned to look him in the face. "You see what I mean now? This is the work of the guild," Jennifer said while pointing at the dismembered corpse. The head, arms, and legs were lying in a pile next to the larger piece of the body.

"Exactly what do you expect us to do, Jennifer? There are no witnesses who know or saw anything. So, who are we going to arrest?" Director Stevens replied trying to hide his irritation.

"They are assassins. If they mention their names, they hunt them down and kill them. Besides, they are wearing suits, gloves, and masks to cover their entire body. Their outfits keep them hidden in plain sight and helps them not leave forensic evidence behind," Jennifer informed him.

Wade nodded. "Fair enough, Jenn. But I really think you're putting us in over our heads and pay rate if we are dealing with real live assassins. You do remember what happened to the last group of agents working such a case, do you not?" Director Stevens said warningly.

"And do you not find it strange that Agents Tabitha Greene and Saki Po were the only agents to live?" Jennifer shot back defiantly.

The director sighed out of frustration. "Are you accusing two highly decorated agents who retired from the bureau of being members of an assassin's guild?" he asked.

By the tone of his voice, Jennifer realized what he was trying to get her to understand. Even if she was right about her accusations, who would believe her? The look on the other agents' faces made it perfectly clear that no one was buying it.

'All this hard work for nothing,' she thought.

Jennifer had personally lured the homeless man into the dark alleyway around 12 a.m., and she'd done all the malicious dismembering herself after slitting his throat with a sword Tabitha kept inside of the utility closet. *'Fine, I'll do it myself,'* she thought. "I understand what you're saying, Director Stevens."

"Thanks, Jenn. No need of losing more good agents to a ghost hunt," he replied.

"You're absolutely correct. I'll use my own resources to investigate and bring them down," Jennifer said, her voice full of determination.

Wade nonchalantly shrugged his shoulders. "I cannot tell you what not to do with your own resources and time, Jennifer. As long as you do not attempt to use the bureau's finances or database for your own selfish reasons."

"In layman terms, do not look for any assistance from you? Have a great day, Wade," Jennifer said before storming off.

Wade shook his head in disbelief. He watched her get in the 911 Porsche and speed off before pulling his Galaxy S10 out and making a phone call. The phone rang twice before the line was connected.

"Hello?" the man answered on the other end.

"It is Diablo, brother," Wade replied.

The line was silent for a moment. "What's good, Master Diablo? Is everything alright?" the man asked.

Wade walked off a pace, making sure no one was eavesdropping on his conversation. "It's Jennifer, she is adamant about bringing your family and the Po Clan down. She is launching her own private investigation."

The man's voice became full of laughter. Not that he found the information funny. It was the person behind it that humored him. "If she is bent on chasing her own death, then let her. She'll find what she's looking for."

Willie Slaughter

Chapter One

"10-4, brother," Wade replied and hung up the phone. He stepped back over to the crime scene and gave orders for the scene to be cleaned up. One of the agents pulled him to the side away from the other two.

"Master Diablo, what should we do about Jennifer? She is becoming a nuisance," the agent said showing her irritation.

Agent Beatrice Soledad was brown-skinned, with long, silky, black hair, 31 years old, 5'8 and 148 pounds. She was mixed with African and Indian descent. Although an agent within the bureau, she was also an assassin whose code name was Chalice.

"We do nothing unless she crosses our path, Chalice," he replied.

They walked back over to the other two agents. "Agents Grant and Smiley, it is your show. Agent Soledad and I have to get back to the office."

They continued to collect DNA samples from around the scene. Wade and Beatrice got in the unmarked Sedan and drove off.

***

Trent's flight landed and he stepped out onto the solid ground. Man, it feels good to be back home, he thought to himself as he grabbed the duffle bag from the baggage cart and stepped onto the escalator. He went down into the terminal and sat, waiting on the Amtrak train to come. Knowing the schedule, he found himself purchasing a newspaper and catching up on the happenings in New Jersey City.

Although he was glad to be home, Trent missed Malice and Angel already. He even began to miss Tabitha. "With her aggravating ass," he thought out loud before he knew it. The statement alone made him laugh.

Finally, the Amtrak train came coasting to a complete stop in the terminal. Trent, not wanting to be bothered with bumping into people trying to hurry on to get the seat of their choice, made a beeline for the open passenger door. He sat in the back near the window, so he could see the view while riding to his destination. As the train moved forward and out of the terminal into the morning light, he relaxed. He watched the people bustling back and forth on the sidewalks heading to and from work and the peddlers hustle their goods on the Jersey streets.

Trent sighed seeing the prostitutes working the streets. It was a terrible sight in his eyes, but it was a part of the streets of Jersey. His home, and to him, there was no place better.

The Amtrak train pulled into another terminal and came to a stop. Trent made his way through the crowd of passengers, saying excuse me as politely as he could until he was off the train. He relaxed again once he was not feeling overcrowded. Crowds just were not his thing.

Trent walked over to a drink machine. Thankfully, it carried bottled water. He bought a bottle of spring water before getting on the escalator, riding it to the topside of Jersey City. As he drank the water, he had an eerie feeling like he was being watched or even followed.

'That's Jersey for you, someone's always watching you, especially a black man carrying a duffle bag,' he thought as he continued to drink the water. The escalator took him to the sidewalk directly across from his townhouse.

As he made his way across the street, the eerie feeling of being watched tugged at him again. But at seeing his neighbor sitting on her front porch, Trent dismissed the thought and waved. "Hi, Miranda. How have you been?" he said with a smile.

"Well, look who decided to return to Jersey. I've been lonely, but good. How about yourself, Trent?" Miranda replied.

Miranda was mixed Puerto Rican and black. She was 28 years old, 5'2, 130 pounds, brown-skinned, with long, silky, black hair that she wore in two braids and hazel brown eyes. To top it off, she did not have any children. She'd moved in the neighborhood a month after Trent, and they would have conversations occasionally.

Trent was very fond of Miranda, but the lifestyle he lived kept him from pursuing the relationship he wanted with her. Instead of walking on over to his house, which sat right next to hers, he found himself stepping up on her front porch and having a seat.

"Queen, you sound like you missed a brother," Trent said.

Miranda nodded. "Yup, I did. But, let's keep it real. You never showed any interest in me, Trent. So, does it really matter?"

Trent frowned. "Yes, it does matter. It is not that I'm not interested in you, Queen. It is the life I live."

"Champagne, that's understandable if that's the case. So, where you been?" she said.

"Beijing, China," he replied.

Miranda sat upright in the chair. "Damn, when you disappear, you disappear for real. Did you enjoy your trip?"

Trent shook his head. "No, it was not that kind of flight. It was strictly business. And no, I did not enjoy being away from our daily conversations. I missed you too, Miranda."

She sucked her teeth and waved him off. "Yeah, whatever. Tell me anything just because you know I'm feeling you."

Trent slid his chair around so he could look into her hazel brown eyes. "Seriously, Queen, I'm ready to pursue my happiness. Let's live the rest of this lifetime and the next together."

Miranda swallowed hard, staring into his eyes, she knew he was being serious about them being together. "Alright, King. So, which one of our houses are we turning into our home?"

"I was thinking on the tip of selling and moving into a more suitable environment for a family," Trent replied.

Miranda was about to respond when Trent's house phone started ringing. "Seems like someone was looking forward to you coming back home," she said.

Trent looked towards the townhouse. "Probably Ken and Angela calling to make sure I made it back safe and sound. They got married while we were over there. It was a fly ceremony."

"Sounds like the kind you want," she replied.

Trent shrugged his shoulders. "Do not make me book us a first-class flight out for tomorrow morning," he teased but was serious. "Well, let me go answer this phone because whoever's calling isn't stopping."

"Okay, King, I'll see you after you get settled in," Miranda said.

As Trent took a step off the porch, the phone stop ringing. To him, it was a good thing because he did not want to end their conversation. He sat back down next to Miranda. "Well, that—" Before he could get the rest of the sentence out, the explosion happened.

As the window panes shattered, bursting out onto the front, back and side lawn, Trent's townhouse went up in flames. "What in the hell just happened?" he thought out loud. He looked at Miranda, who he quickly realized was in a state of shock.

"Miranda?!" he yelled while shaking her by the shoulders. Seeing it was useless, Trent picked her up and carried her inside of her house. He laid her on the couch before taking out his cellphone and making a phone call.

Sun's phone rung until it went to voicemail. That's when realization kicked in. Trent had forgotten the difference within the timeframe between New Jersey and China. Still, he left a voicemail before hanging up.

Trent sat the phone on the coffee table. Looking into Miranda's eyes, seeing the faraway gaze, he dropped on his knees before her. He calmed himself, putting his own concerns aside for the moment to do what he needed to do. Once he felt his breath and heartbeat was back aligned, he gently touched Miranda's left temple with his right index and forefinger while touching his with his left.

Trent closed his eyes and deepened his concentration until he felt the flow of energy flowing between them. Feeling the slight jolt of her body, he opened his eyes and stood up before her eyelids fluttered open. Miranda sat up on the couch with a look of pure confusion on her face.

"How did I get on the couch? I could've sworn we were sitting on the front porch kicking it. What's up, Poppy?" she said.

Trent threw his hands up, allowing the frustration to return, and flopped down on the couch next to her. "Miranda, you went into shock, so I carried you inside."

She frowned. "But why?"

"Because someone blew my goddam house up. Now, I have to find somewhere to stay until I can find another house on the market," Trent replied.

"What do you mean, you got to find somewhere to stay? Trent, you're staying with me. That's final," Miranda demanded.

"I do not think that's a good idea, Miranda. I cannot put your life in danger like that," Trent shot back.

"Poppy, I hear what you're saying, but fuck that. We are in this together. You said you are ready to be my king, so it is what it is. Get yourself settled in. I got to go to work," she said and jumped up off the couch.

Trent sat and watched her walk off towards the backroom. His thoughts were running a thousand miles per second, but the sway of her hips slowed them down. *'Man, I got to get this shit done and over with fast,'* he thought.

Miranda came walking back through the living room dressed in a loosely fitting women's canary yellow business pants suit. "Make sure you're here when I get home, Trent," she said before walking out the door.

Not a good five minutes after she had left, the sounds of the fire truck and patrol car sirens blared. There was no need of looking to find out where they were going. Trent unzipped the duffle bag, took out something to wear, and went to take a shower. While showering, he listened to the thunderous roar of the water putting out the fire next door, and his thoughts were centered around finding out who did it and ending their life or lives.

Chapter Two

Jennifer had not been there to see whether Trent was caught in the explosion. She had a good feeling that he was because she had watched him ride the escalator up to the street directly across from his townhouse. In her mind, he probably went straight in and jumped in the shower. More of the explanation to why he did not answer the phone when she had called.

'It would have been better to hear his voice before the explosion killed him,' Jennifer thought while sitting across the street from where the firemen and police worked to get control of the burning townhouse.

She had a dark blue hoodie on just in case someone came around who knew her and just in case Trent had somehow survived the blast. She had paid the demolition expert to wire the explosives so it would detonate ten seconds after Trent answered the phone or after the third time, she tried to call. It ended up being a free job because she seduced him into her bedroom when he came to collect the payment and stabbed him in the chest repeatedly with one of Tabitha's daggers.

Jennifer covered the bed in plastic to make sure the blood did not stain or soak into the mattresses. The covers she used ended up in the fireplace. She was proving to be just as good at killing and getting away with it, as those who she wanted dead. She was confident Trent was dead.

"One down. Oh, Tabitha Greene, you're going to wish you stayed with me," Jennifer said at a whisper while riding back down the escalator.

***

Morning came, and everyone on the Sune Compound participated in the morning ritual. The elder, Ty Po led them in the meditation. Afterward, everyone departed silently to their living quarters and washed up for the morning meal. Sun and Shyan showered together and made love while at it.

On their way out, Sun noticed the miss calls and voicemail modifications lit up on the screen of his cellphone. Due to the fact that he could not verbally speak to whoever had left the message, he left it unread until after the morning meal. Side by side, he and his wife walked over into the dining hall, where majority of the Po and Sune Clan were already seated, waiting on breakfast to be served.

As normal, breakfast consisted of different styled cooked salmon, deep-fried rice paddies, waffles, raw honey syrup, and hot, mint leaf tea. A breakfast fit for royalty. After they ate and the table was cleared of the leftovers and dirty dishes, the casual conversing began around the table. Sun, remembering the notifications on his iPhone, excused himself and walked out with Shyan following close behind him.

They entered their room and grabbed their phones, checking messages, voicemail and miss calls. Shyan did not have any of the above, but Sun did. He had a miss call from Trent and voicemail to go along with it.

"Trent must've made it back to Jersey yesterday," Sun said looking at the time, it was 10:15 a.m.

"What makes you say that, bae?" asked Shyan, who put her Galaxy S10 down on the night light table and laid across the bed rubbing her stomach. She was full.

"He called and left a voicemail," Sun replied.

Shyan sat up on the side of the bed, interested in hearing the voicemail. "Let's hear what bro had to say."

He put the phone on speakerphone as he played the voicemail, *"Peace, bro! Man, shit just got real! Someone just blew my fucking house up! I'm good, though, but I'm about to find out who tried to detonate me. You know what's up when I do! Chop! Chop! Tell my favorite sister, Angela, I said peace and love! Get at me when you get this message! Peace!"*

It was like time stood still in the room. Sun and Shyan sat speechless. Sun played the recording over and over again. His anger rising every time.

"Baby, he's fine," Shyan said as she grabbed the phone and turned off the voicemail.

"We got to go. I mean we got to go now," Sun said and started packing. Shyan did not ask questions. She started packing her things as well. While they were bustling about the room gathering their belongings, a knock came to the room door.

"Come in!" Sun yelled, his voice full of frustration and anger. His mind was really filled with malicious thoughts.

Moon Tao Po, Saki, Yishi, and Sia entered the room and bowed. Although they were filled with determination to leave, Sun and Shyan stopped packing and returned the respect. Moon, being very observant, realized something must have just transpired for them to be packing.

"Masters Sun and Shyan Sune, for what reasons are you packing? Is there trouble?" asked Moon Tao Po.

Neither responded. Shyan, on the other hand, picked up Sun's phone and played the voicemail on speakerphone for them to hear. Moon, Saki, Yishi, and Sia listened quietly. After playing the recording twice, Shyan turned the phone back off and put it in her front pocket.

"I've never been to America before. I guess now is a better time than ever to take a trip," Yishi said.

Shyan and Sun returned to their packing. "If you're planning on catching the flight with us, you better start packing," Sun said while stuffing the last of his clothing inside of one of the open duffle bags on the bed.

Yishi took a seat in the chair next to the red oak wood dresser. "Well, Master Sun Sune, it is not that simple. We must take the matter before the elders first. There's no doubt that they will consent to our departure to go, aide, a kindred spirit."

Done packing, Shyan zipped up the duffle bags. As much as she did not want to admit, she knew Yishi was right. "Baby, Master Yishi Sune is speaking the truth. It is custom to take all matters such as this before the elders."

Sun hefted one duffle bag strap onto his right shoulder and carried the other by the strap in his left hand. "Time is ticking. Let's go talk to the elders, so we can leave. The sooner, the better," he said and walked out of the room followed by Shyan. Yishi, Saki, Sia, and Moon fell in step behind them.

The group made their way across the compound to Ma Sune's study. Instead of stopping at the door that led into the study, Yishi ushered them straight down the hallway towards the high double doors at the end of the hall. She pushed the doors inward and walked inside, announcing their arrival. Ma, Mae, Nya and the other elders ceased in their conversations at the announcement.

"Master Yishi Sune, what brings you here at this hour of the sun?" asked Ma Sune. She could feel the energy emanating from them and immediately knew something was wrong. "What's wrong, my child? Speak."

Like the last time, Shyan stepped forward with Sun's phone and played the voicemail on speakerphone before the elders. They all gathered around the table to listen. While it played,

Sun remained posted up against the wall near the doors when it hit him.

"That bitch!" he exclaimed out loud, thinking he was saying it in his mind. He tried to cover his mouth, but it was too late.

Everyone's attention went to him. The only person used to seeing him upset or to ever hear him use profanity in such a manner was Shyan. It was the others first time, so it had a startling effect.

"Master Sun Sune, I beg your pardon. Would you care to share your revelation with the rest of us?" Mae said.

Sun nodded. "First, I would like to apologize for the use of such language in the presence of my elders and women." He turned his gaze toward Moon Tao Po and continued to speak, "Right after Jennifer returned to America. I received a call from a reliable source. They informed me of Jennifer's acts of vengeance towards the guild and Po Clan. To put simply, she'd filed a report to her superiors at the Federal Bureau in Jersey, which ended up getting the slaughterhouse raided."

"What?" Moon interjected before she knew it. It was obvious to her that Jennifer her ex-lover, called herself getting back at her for leaving her.

"So, they found death everywhere. No pressure there, though. That was cleaned up and swept under the rug so to speak. But it seems Jennifer has decided to take matters into her own hands," Sun said.

"That's it I'm going to take care of this, right now," an angry Moon Tao Po said while storming off in the direction of the doors. Sia and Shyan, knowing what was on her mind, quickly blocked her path. "What are y'all doing? Get out of my way," she demanded, but neither budged.

"Master Moon Tao Po, what you intend to do will no doubt kill you. The distance is too great, and your emotions are imbalanced. Not saying you will not reach your destination and complete the task. However, you wouldn't make it back. So, it is not an option," Shyan stated.

Seeing it would be of no use to argue, Moon Tao Po posted up against the wall beside her cousin, Sun Sune.

"Okay," Ma Sune said to get everybody's attention before she continued to speak, "Here's my strategy view. Masters Saki and Sia, neither of you must go on this journey because your presence would be noticed. Master Yishi, take Qi Dom Po and Yuri and accompany Masters Shyan, Sun and Moon."

Her daughter nodded and left the room to go pack and inform Qi and Yuri of the mission. In Yishi's absence, Ma Sune made a few phone calls to arrange their flight. When Yishi returned fifteen minutes later with Qi Dom Po and Yuri at her sides, the elder Ty Po took the floor.

"Young Masters, before you all make this journey, let me send you on your way with these words of wisdom. As warriors of the way of Ninja, you must recognize and understand the sufferings of others. To do so, you shall begin to understand their ways and their boundaries. It is the only way to truly defeat your opponent.

"Moreover, for a brief reminder of history, recall that we are all descendants of the greatest warriors. The Shang Dynasty. The Po Clan being the closest of this lineage to still live. At all times, there must be the awareness of being engaged in the constant never-ending development of self-defense built by the Black Dragon and Green Mantis Spirits and on their spiritual principles. Again, another important lesson to overcome and truly defeat your opponent.

"In the sun and moon of old, you would have had to go through a rite of passage to become and be recognized as a warrior of the way of Ninja. The journey was a loner's journey to travel. There were several who did not make it back. The sun could not guide you, nor could the moon shield you from the dangers to be encountered while going through the rite of passage," Ty Po said. He stood up and walked over to stand directly in front of Sun.

"When you return from your journey, this rite of passage shall await you," Ty Po said.

Sun bowed. "Master Ty Po, I will honor you and all of the ancestors by accepting the task."

Ma Sune clapped her hands loudly, which got everyone's attention. "Great. Now, to inform you of your flight arrangement. You'll be taking my private jet, so feel free to take whatever you know is needed. And the pilot will remain at a motel, therefore, once you're done, you can board the flight and be on your way back. May the spirit of the Black Dragon and Green Mantis accompany you on your journey," Ma Sune said.

Sun, Shyan, Yuri, Yishi, Qi, and Moon left. Neither said goodbye because they all felt like goodbyes meant there was a chance of no return. They gathered everything they planned to take into one of the SUVs and headed for the private airstrip.

Willie Slaughter

Chapter Three

Ma Sune's thoughts went to her young lover, Zhia Mi Yang. She excused herself, went to her study, and called Zhia. She answered on the second ring. They talked about the weather and business for a moment. Before the call ended plans were made for Ma to meet her down at the docks so they could spend some quality time together.

"I'll be on my way shortly, Master Zhia Mi Yang," Ma Sune said.

"And I'll be waiting, lover. But before we leave, I have to make my rounds," Zhia replied, remembering every time she left the office on unofficial business she had to do a full dock check to make sure everything was operating properly and the workers were not in need of anything.

"No problem. We shall make the rounds together," Ma Sune said and hung up.

She grabbed her sword and left the study. Normally, she would announce her leaving the compound, but not this time. This time, Ma Sune jumped in her forest green 500 Mercedes Benz and left. Traffic was moving at a rather fast pace, so the drive along the way end up being short.

Ma Sune arrived at the docks twenty minutes later. She parked right out front of the main office building and got out. Zhia saw her walking towards the office entrance and hurried out to meet and greet her.

"It is good to see you, Master Ma Sune," Zhia said, looking her over. Ma Sune was dressed in a simple green silk full-length body dress that hugged her frame nicely.

"And so, do you, Master Zhia Mi Yang," she complimented. Zhia had on a gold and black tiger stripe body dress that fit her petite frame perfectly.

"Thank you," Zhia replied. "Let us make the rounds, so we can go have some fun. I'm dying to taste you."

The two women started walking towards the loading and unloading area. Ma Sune watched while Zhia read over documents and signed them. There was more paperwork that had to be handled when dealing with the export goods than the import. Looking at some of the cargo crates, Ma Sune's thoughts went to the moment they'd found the children inside of the cargo.

"Has there been any more trouble with any shipments?" asked Ma Sune as they walked down the plank from the cargo ship.

"Yes, some. About a week ago, Jun Yang discovered three boys, ages nine, ten and twelve, inside a crate. They were on the brink of starvation. I turned them over to the local authorities along with the usual amounts of drugs found," Zhia replied.

Ma Sune shook her head out of disgust. "I guess the last message was not clear enough."

"Or they thought they were exempt. I have the shipment documents in my office," Zhia said.

They walked, taking in casual conversation on their way to Zhia's office. Inside, Zhia rummaged through the bottom drawer of the file cabinet next to her desk until she found the two files she was looking for. "Here they are," she said as she handed the two manilla folders to Ma Sune.

Ma Sune opened and glanced over the first file. It was the documents for the drug shipment. She closed it quickly because it was not any of her immediate concern. The second file was of interest to her.

Ma Sune sat on the corner of Zhia's desk while she read the documented report of the finding of the three boys concealed within the cargo belonging to Lee's Rice Industries. But, undercover, the Lee Clan also owned sweatshops all over China. Their master, Tien Fu Lee's signature was on the documents.

"I think we should pay Master Tien Fu Lee a visit," Ma said.

Zhia shrugged her shoulders. "Okay. According to the delivery address on the documents, the shipment was to be delivered to their main sweatshop compound. I know exactly where it is located."

"Aren't they the Grey Rhino Clan?" asked Ma Sune.

Zhia nodded. "Yes, an undisciplined clan at that."

"Then there's no need of taking any extra help. We can handle this alone," Ma Sune replied.

Zhia grabbed her two short swords. "Let's go. We can take my car."

Zhia and Ma Sune walked out of the office. Zhia locked the door to the office behind her before they made their way to her gold Mitsubishi Eclipse that had a Siberian Tiger painted on the hood. They got in, with Zhia behind the wheel, and left the docks. The drive to their destination was a short drive, so it did not give them much time to talk.

"There is the entrance to the sweatshop compound," Zhia said while nodding in the direction of a gated driveway, where there was a guard's outpost with two guards dressed in grey uniforms. "It would be easier if we walk in instead of drive. That way if we leave anyone alive, nobody can say they saw what we were riding in."

"Great thinking, Master Zhia Mi Yang," Ma Sune said as a compliment.

Zhia parked on the dirt road a couple of yards down from the sweatshop compound's entrance. It was an empty lot surrounded by trees. They got out with their swords latched onto belts around their waists that Zhia provided.

"This is going to throw our quality time off, my lover. I guess we should consider dinner at my place," Zhia said while they walked down the road, heading for the gates.

Ma Sune did not respond because she had already considered it and had plans to have dinner at Zhia's house. As they approached the locked gates, the two guards positioned themselves in front of them. Neither said a word. They just stared as if waiting for Zhia and Ma Sune to show some identification.

"Greetings. We are here to make special orders concerning a few ideal dresses," Zhia said, sounding professional.

The male guard who stood to the left of Zhia eyed her closely. Not for suspicious reasons, but lustfulness. In his eyes, both of them were beautiful women looking for some fine fabrics to show off their curvaceous bodies. He nudged his comrade in the side. "Move out of the way. Let the women through," he commanded in Mandarin.

The other guard hurried inside the outpost and pressed the button. The electronic gates slid open just wide enough to allow them entrance. Both Zhia and Ma Sune bowed respectfully before walking through the open gates.

"Piece of cake," Zhia said. She and Ma Sune quickly began surveying the area. There were at least three Grey Rhinos, wearing the smoke grey ninja suits, posted at the entrance of every sweatshop.

"Yes, we are definitely having dinner at your home," Ma Sune said, seeing the Grey Rhinos.

Zhia did not reply. She looked around as if to be trying to remember the layout. All of a sudden, the memory came back.

"Now, I remember. The main building is this way," she said and started walking in the direction she pointed in.

Ma Sune stayed at her side. The solemn faces of the workers who hustled and bustled back and forth caught her attention. She realized they were not paid workers but forced laborers who were sold through human trafficking. The thought caused Ma Sune to grip the hilt of her sword firmer.

They came to a building sitting off from the rest. "Yes, this is the right building," Zhia said as they walked inside.

"Good," Ma Sune began to say. She had to check the time before continuing, "Afternoon," she completed the greeting at the secretary's desk, which was a charred wooden desk.

The elderly woman did not even look up from her task. She did not even respond right off. She clicked on a few more keys to finish the report first. "How may I assist you?" she asked without making eye contact.

To Ma Sune, it was a show of disrespect. But, since the mission they were on was to eliminate the Grey Rhino, she set it aside for the moment. However, she still let Zhia do the talking, knowing she had nothing nice to say.

"Of course. We are here to meet with Master Tien Fu Lee. Is the master available?" Zhia said.

The secretary shook her head. "No, Master Tien Fu Lee is not here."

"Very well. Then we would like to speak with whoever's in charge of this operation," Zhia responded.

"That will be Master Jun Joa Lee. Master Tien Fu Lee's son. He's available. The third office door down the hall on the right," the secretary replied. Then another thought hit her, and that's when she finally looked up at Zhia and Ma Sune. "I must forewarn you Master Jun Joa Lee has a sexual appetite for pretty women such as yourself. Do not be surprised if you are interrupting something. Aye?" she said while winking her right eye at Zhia.

Although disgusted from the thought of it, Zhia allowed the illusion of a smile to play across her lips. "Understood. We shall be very discreet about our business affair," she replied before her and Ma Sune began walking in the direction the secretary gave.

They walked down the hallway. Once they were out of sight of the secretary, they stopped and unsheathed their swords. When they reached the door to Jun Joa Lee's office, Ma Sune tried the lock. It was open.

She eased the door open and walked on inside of the office. Zhia brought up the rear and eased the office door back shut. Just like the secretary had forewarned them, Jun had a young teenage girl, who could not have been older than thirteen, naked in his lap bouncing up and down on top of him like there was no tomorrow. He groaned and grunted loudly while she barely made a sound.

Jun had his chair turned facing the wall, so he did not see them standing in front of his desk. But, the teenage girl could, and she did. While riding him hard and fast, her eyelids fluttered open. She was about to speak, but Ma Sune held a finger to her lips, gesturing for her to remain silent.

Knowing it would be his last ride, Zhia and Ma Sune allowed them to finish their erotic session. Once Jun released inside of his young lover, she got up and put on a colorful silk robe that she kept open in the front, showing her clean shaved sex and hand size breasts.

"Master Jun Joa Lee?" Zhia said in a commanding tone of voice.

The twenty-two-year-old man whirled around in the chair with a big smile on his face, showing rows of shiny gold with diamond cut teeth. Seeing the two beautiful women standing before him, he stood up, letting them see his nude body and erection. "Yeah, I'm Master Jun Joa Lee. What, you bitches come to fuck?"

"I'm Master Zhia Mi Yang, and this is Master Ma Sune. There was a shipment you were expecting to arrive a few suns ago, but it did not make it through inspection," Zhia said in a professional tone of voice.

"And?" he replied. Jun grabbed his erection and started masturbating. "You two fine bitches. Yeah, look at this hard cock. Come suck and fuck this cock, bitches."

Ma Sune had felt sympathy for the teenage girl. But seeing her sitting on the corner of the desk laughing at Jun's blatant disrespectful gesture and speech, that feeling changed. Her hand gripped the hilt of her sword firmly.

"The three boys and opium were handed over to the authorities by me. You will not be receiving any of your cargo," Zhia said.

Jun continued to masturbate until he spewed his contents on the carpeted floor in front of them. "Ah yeah. You bitches are a good fuck."

Ma Sune had held her composure as long as she could. In one swift movement, she cut his penis off at the testicles. He was about to yell, but she placed the blade that was already stained with his blood to his throat. "Ssshhh, you are making too much noise, be quiet."

Seeing what had happened to her lover, the teenage girl tried to make a run for the door, but Zhia stepped in her path and slashed straight down the center of her body, starting from her forehead. She was dead before her body hit the floor. Her blood soaked into the light grey carpet.

"Now. Where were we?" Zhia said.

Jun was in a state of shock. His eyes were glued to his penis laying on the floor before him. Zhia could not help but smirk.

"Jun Joa Lee, you will not miss it. It was not like it was pleasing anyone. Even the little girl was not pleased by it," Zhia said sarcastically.

Jun's fearful expression turned cold and callous. "How dare you bitches come into my place and insult my manhood. You will not make it out of here alive. And I'll have thirty little boys to take the place of the three. You whores do not know who you fucking with. My—" Before he could get the words out of his mouth, Ma Sune severed his head from his body with one stroke of her blade.

"Well, that is that," she said as she wiped the bloodstained blade on the robe of the dead girl.

Zhia and Ma Sune walked out of the room, closing the door behind them. It had become quiet inside the building, so they crept down the hallway staying close to the wall. Ma Sune peeped around the corner and saw that the secretary was no longer sitting at the desk.

"It is obvious they have an ambush in place for us. Are you ready?" Ma Sune whispered.

In response to the question, Zhia nodded her head. They stepped from around the corner to stand in the open space. Just as they had known, the ambush was there. Ten Grey Rhinos surrounded them with their weapons ready at hand.

Zhia and Ma Sune did not wait on them to make the first move. The two deadly warriors launched an all-out attack on the opposition. Their superior skills were unmatched. They slaughtered the ten within a minute's timeframe.

Barely breathing hard and with blood dripping from the blades of their swords, Zhia and Ma Sune stared into each other's eyes. Before either realized it, they were sharing a passionate kiss. Neither desiring to end the moment, but both knowing there was more bloodshed to happen before they would truly be able to enjoy each other's company for the remainder of the day.

"I could make love to you, right now," Ma Sune said as she pulled away from the kiss.

Zhia hatched her dress up, revealing she was not wearing any panties and sat up on top of the secretary's desk. "What's stopping you?" she asked while removing the shoulder straps and bra.

Ma Sune stood in between her thighs and started kissing her around the neck while massaging her breasts with her right hand and fingering her with her left hand. Zhia moaned and spread her legs wider to receive the pleasure in full that her lover was giving. She thrust herself hard and fast onto Ma Sune's fingers. Her lips trembled from the sensation building up within the coming release.

Ma Sune showered her breasts with passionate kisses. She sucked and pulled on Zhia's erect nipples while rubbing her clitoris faster and faster in a circular motion. It was not long before Zhia's body began to shake as her release came with the building heat and wetness between her thighs. Her release came in squirts.

"Oh, Ma. You always get all of me," Zhia said while straightening out her dress.

"This is only the beginning of a long moon," Ma Sune replied.

Both women retrieved their swords from the dead bodies they'd thrust the blades in before giving themselves over to their intimate thoughts. Zhia peeped out of the only window inside of the building and noticed the secretary talking to a group of Grey Rhinos dressed in grey ninja suits while pointing towards the building. The group unsheathed their swords and started walking in the direction of the main office.

"We have more company coming to join the ranks of the dead," Zhia said while keeping her eyes on the approaching assassins. It was eighteen of them approaching the front entrance.

"Let them come. We will give them a warm welcome with the blade of our swords," Ma Sune replied and readied herself. She stood out in the opening, so they would see her as soon as they entered the front door. Zhia stood opposite of the way the door would open for a surprise attack.

The door swung open, and they charged in, directing their line of attack straight for Ma Sune. The last person to enter was the secretary. When she cleared the doorway, Zhia kicked the door closed before thrusting the blade, all the way to the hilt, through her lower spine. She pushed the woman's lifeless corpse off the blade.

Having the eighteen assassins in between them, Zhia and Ma Sune began the slaughter. Without breaking stride or sweat, they ended the lives of their foes. The two masters met up in the middle of a pile of death and bowed respectfully to each other.

"I could do this with you forever, Master Ma Sune," Zhia said.

"As we will, Master Zhia Mi Yang," Ma Sune replied.

They made their way around the sweatshop compound, slaughtering every Grey Rhino. Once there were none left to kill, the two women had a discussion with the enslaved workers, telling them they were free to go or stay and keep the fabric business going for themselves.

"If you choose to stay and run this business, we promise our protection of your lives and livelihood," Zhia stated. Everyone resigned to stay and make a living for themselves and family.

On their way back out the gates of the compound, Zhia and Ma Sune slaughtered the two guards on post. Before they left, Ma Sune made a phone call to her compound, demanding that some reinforcements be sent to keep guard over the sweatshop compound. She had every intention of keeping her word to the people working there. They waited for them to get there before leaving from the front entrance.

"Now, we can have our quality time," Zhia said as she sat behind the wheel of her car. She backed out of the parking place and drove off.

At Zhia's place, they showered together, washing away the stench of death, and they made love during the process. Afterward, they walked down the stairs into the kitchen and decided what kind of meal they would prepare together. They settled for a simple dish of fried whole-grain noodles and salmon with a mixture of spices. Neither wore anything.

Willie Slaughter

Chapter Four

Jennifer signed for the FedEx package. She gave the deliveryman a generous tip. She was tied between wanting to open the package and waiting until after work to open it. Due to the fact she had a whole hour before she had to be at the federal building's entrance, she decided to go ahead and open it.

"Just magnificent!" she exclaimed after unwrapping the package, laying the off-white ninja suit on the bed and taking a step back. Not that she was a ninja, but Jennifer knew she had to start thinking like one in order to get her revenge on Tabitha.

Jennifer resolved to getting herself ready for work. She was on her way out the front door when she remembered she had not taken her medicine. Quickly, she ran back into the bathroom adjoined to the master bedroom and opened the medicine cabinet. She took two pills out of the bottle and took them.

Jennifer grimaced from the sour taste it put in her mouth. *'A small price to pay for living to get revenge,'* she thought while walking back through the house and out the door. She decided to drive Tabitha's Audi 8 to work. In her mind, it was her car since Tabitha chose to leave.

Dangerously In Love came on the radio while she drove through the slow-moving traffic. It was her and Tabitha's song. Jennifer was having mixed emotions. Before she turned off the radio, the tears were already pouring down her cheeks.

"Tabby, you have to be the stupidest bitch in the world to think you could play with my heart. I'm going to show you what dangerously in love is about." Jennifer thought out loud. She turned off onto the exit leading to her job. Three minutes later, she was at the front entrance, going through security clearance checks.

Normally, Jennifer would park in the garage, but not today. She was all showy. Since Trent's townhouse explosion, hoping that he burned to death inside, gave her a new attitude that was visible in every step she took in the Ralph Lauren's crimson red six-inch heels and business skirt suit to match.

"Good morning, Agent Santiago. How are you doing this awesome morning?" asked Jennifer.

Agent Juan Santiago was a longtime friend of Jennifer's. He was one of the most muscular Latinos she'd ever seen. At 61, 216 pounds, dark brown eyes, and a low fade haircut, Juan Santiago was a gentle giant when it came to friends, family and the ladies.

"I'm doing great, Jenn. What has you all springy? Something in the coffee or in the bedroom?" Juan said grinning.

Jennifer's smile diminished quickly. "Unfortunately, neither. Do not forget about our little get together for lunch."

Juan cocked his head to the side, frowning. He'd already forgotten. "What get together?"

"Just stop by my station before you head out for lunch. I'll refresh your memory along the way. How about that?" Jennifer replied before walking off.

"Okay!" Juan yelled after her. His eyes were glued on the sway of Jennifer's hips. *'Man, I got to figure out a way to tap that ass one time,'* he thought.

Jennifer knew Juan was eyeing her sexually but was not bothered by it. To her, his sexual appetite for her would be to her advantage. She giggled at a thought that crossed her mind as she rounded the corner. The secretary she was relieving was glad to see her coming.

"Jenn, girl, you're on time when I most need you to be," the lady said. She began gathering her belongings to go home.

Jennifer plopped down in the chair, logged into her account, and clocked in. Afterward, she swirled around in the chair to face the woman she was relieving. "Is everything good, Tatiana? Anything I can help you with?" asked Jennifer. She eyed Tatiana from head to toe. She was wearing a peach Women's Polo Skirt suit with open-toe six-inch heels to match.

Tatiana was 55, weighed 139 pounds with her weight in all the right places, short natural hair and dark brown skin and eyes. She knew what kind of lifestyle Jennifer lived. It was hard not knowing because she swung that way every now and then. But there was something about Jennifer that kept her at bay.

"No, I'm good. I appreciate the offer, though. I'll see you at shift change," Tatiana replied and hurried off.

Jennifer watched her walk off. The way the skirt hugged Tatiana's curves had her hypnotized. She wanted to taste her, and she was not going to be denied. Before she realized what, she was doing, Jennifer was on her feet walking at a fast pace to catch her before she reached the elevator.

"Wait up a sec," Jennifer said as she slid inside the closing elevator door.

When the door closed and the elevator began moving, Jennifer hit the emergency stop button, causing the elevator to stop.

"What are you doing, Jenn?" asked Tatiana. She was nervous.

"Just go with the flow," Jennifer replied. She pressed up against Tatiana, pushing her up against the wall of the elevator. Her lips started roaming about her neckline while her hands found their way up Tatiana's skirt.

At first, Tatiana tried to buck against her lustful and aggressive touch. But once Jennifer's fingers found their way inside of her, she ceased to fight and gave in to the pleasure. "Umm, yes," Tatiana moaned.

Jennifer stopped working her magic for a moment to stare into her eyes. "I promise you I will not hurt you, Tatiana. Relax. Just go with the flow."

"Okay, Jenn," she replied.

Jennifer descended to her knees and lifted Tatiana's skirt up to her waistline and spread her legs wide. She sighed, smelling the sweet scent of apple cherry. "Relax, baby. Just relax," she said before thrusting her tongue inside of her sex.

Tatiana moaned uncontrollably. She held on tightly to the guard rail and placed her left leg up on the rail, giving Jennifer all the access to her sex as she wanted. Jennifer licked, kissed and sucked on her clitoris hungrily.

"Oh, Jenn! Jenn! Jenn!" Tatiana screamed. She began rotating her hips, thrusting her sex onto Jennifer's tongue and lips. It was not long before her body started trembling and the release, she'd been longing for happened.

Tasting the sweetness of her release, Jennifer moaned. "Yummy," she said as she stood back to her feet. She helped Tatiana straighten her skirt out and kissed her passionately afterward. "Hopefully, we can continue this another time. Are you down, Tatiana?"

Tatiana kissed her back. "We will see. Until then, think about me."

Jennifer released the emergency brakes of the elevator. "Tasting like that, how can I not think about you?"

She rode down to the parking garage with Tatiana. They made small talk along the way. After they kissed and hugged,

Tatiana went her way and Jennifer took the elevator back up to her workstation.

The first half of the day went by pretty fast for Jennifer. There were not many calls coming in. Juan Santiago was on his way over to her desk when the director came out of his office and requested her presence within his office immediately. She told Juan to wait on her before she did as commanded.

"Yes, sir." She stepped into his office and said.

Wade had sat back down at his desk. Unlike usual when he summoned someone to his office, Jennifer realized he had company. Agent Beatrice Soledad stood next to his desk with her arms crossed comfortably over her breast.

"Agent Soledad, how are you?" Jennifer asked and turned her attention back to Wade. "What's going on, Director Stevens? Has there been a breakthrough?"

Wade sighed. "See, that's just it, Jenn. There will be no breakthrough because there are no witnesses to any of the crimes other than your word of mouth. How are we supposed to investigate a hearsay matter? I'm ordering you to leave well enough alone, Jennifer."

Inside, she was boiling over with rage, but she knew better than showing it on the surface. Jennifer liked her job, and she was definitely out to have something with Tatiana. *'So, why get yourself fired,'* she thought. "Correction, you told me that I could continue to investigate as long as I used my own resources. I'm doing just that, Director Stevens. Now, if that's all you wanted to say, I have a lunch date to attend," Jennifer said with a smile. She thought she saw Beatrice flinch as if she was reaching for something, but when nothing came about the thought was dismissed.

"Alright, Jennifer, have it your way. If your ass bites off more than you can chew, do not think this agency's resources will be used to bail you out. Understood?" the director said.

Jennifer snapped to attention and gave a scout's salute. "Yes, sir."

"You're dismissed," he stated with a wave of his left hand.

Jennifer's ignorance and stupidity were starting to annoy the director and Beatrice. They watched her exit the office and waited until the office door closed behind her before either spoke a word.

"Killing her would almost be senseless and pleasure all in one," Beatrice said while flipping the gold ninja star between her fingers. She had taken it out and concealed it so fast that Jennifer missed it. Her intention was to end Jennifer's life right then, but Wade had tilted his head slightly to the point it was unnoticeable, in a do not do it gesture.

"She'll find death in her own way soon," he replied.

Jennifer stopped by her station to find Juan lounging in her chair half asleep. "Agent, Santiago, let's go," she said startling him. He almost flipped out of the chair. She giggled girlishly and walked off with extra ump in her walk, making her hips sway with a purpose.

Juan jumped to his feet and followed Jennifer down the hall into the elevator.

"Now, what's up, Jenn?" asked Juan.

Knowing where his thoughts were, Jennifer played the part. She pulled him into a kiss but quickly pulled back from him when the thought of the intimate moment she and Tatiana shared in the elevator.

"It is more where that came from if you're buying lunch," she said.

"Where do you want to eat?" asked Juan without hesitation. All he could think about was, fulfilling the longing growing below the waist.

Jennifer checked the time on her Echo Citizen watch. It was 11:58 a.m., meaning, they had a good hour before lunch break was over. "The vegan restaurant on the plaza. Then we can stop by The Marriott if we have enough time."

Agent Santiago looked at the numbers counting down to the garage floor. In his mind, it was not moving fast enough. When they reached the garage floor, he let out a sigh.

"Aren't you ready to rumble?" Jennifer said seductively. "I did not park down under today, so I guess we will be splurging in your Jaguar."

Agent Santiago did not say a word. He led the way to his vehicle, opened and closed the passenger's side door for her before getting behind the wheel, and driving to their first destination.

The plaza was only fifteen minutes away on foot. Driving, about five minutes. Agent Santiago made it in three minutes. He pulled into the plaza's parking lot and parked in front of the vegan restaurant.

"We are here. Are we ordering to go or what?" he said.

Jennifer could hear the impatience within his voice. Due to the fact she needed Juan to handle some unofficial work, she continued to act the part. "To go. We have business to discuss and take care of. Please do not be disappointing on either end, Juan."

Juan responded with a chuckle. They walked the short distance across the parking lot to the restaurant. A lot of pressure was taken away from Juan's mind when he saw the short line of customers waiting to order.

'The day is working out to my advantage after all,' he thought.

Jennifer pondered her course of action. It was already evident that she had to give herself to Juan in exchange for his service and loyalty. *'A small price to pay for revenge,'* she thought. She mentally prepared herself for it while they waited in line.

After ten minutes of waiting in line, they ordered their takeout and was back on the road. Jennifer enjoyed her meal during the drive to their next destination. She was done by the time Juan pulled into The Marriott's parking lot and parked in front of the admission office.

"I'll be right back with the room key," he said as he got out of the car.

Jennifer watched him hurry inside and back out with the quickness. He motioned for her to get out and come on. Back inside the building, they rode the escalator up to the third floor of the five-star hotel. They chatted and laughed on the way to the room.

"Oh my!" Jennifer exclaimed once inside of the suite. It was a luxurious suite. A king-size rotating bed in the middle of the floor, a Jacuzzi sat off to the side, and a mini wine bar to top it off.

Juan threw the key on the minibar countertop. "I wanted the first time to be special, so you will know what is in store every time we get together."

Jennifer looked at the time. It was 12:27 p.m. They had a good twenty minutes to do whatever they were going to do before they had to get back on the road to work. Because it would take them a good thirteen minutes to make it back on time.

"We do not have time for foreplay and talking, Agent Santiago," she said. Jennifer pushed him back onto the bed, which moved like water on contact. "A waterbed. Mm. This is going to be the best quickie of your life."

Juan unfastened his belt and unbuttoned his pants. Jennifer climbed on top of him and started kissing him on the lips as she pulled his penis free of his boxers.

"Yes!" she exclaimed, feeling he was already hard and liking the size of his throbbing sex. She sat up straight and hiked the skirt up around her waistline, revealing the nakedness beneath. Holding his erect shaft with her left hand, Jennifer eased down onto him, moaning through the entire process.

Juan did not know what to do. He grunted and moaned at the tightness of her around him. The moisture between her thighs was so overwhelming to his manhood that he had to restrain himself from releasing.

"Are you ready, Agent Santiago?" asked Jennifer as she rocked back and forth slowly. "Are you ready to cum for me?" She picked up the pace.

"Hell yeah, Mommy! Give it to me," Juan replied, grabbing onto her hips and thrusting up inside of her.

"I need you to do something for me!" Jennifer yelled feeling the pleasure and pain mixed. It had been years since she'd been with a man.

"Whatever you want, Mommy. Just name it," Juan replied. He could not hang on any longer. "Oh, Jenn. Jenn, I'm about to cum."

That she was not about to allow him to do. Jennifer dismounted him, grabbed his throbbing member in her right hand, and jerked him off until he released. Without saying a word, she got up and hurried into the bathroom. Quickly, she took a five-minute shower, got back dressed, and came out of the bathroom smiling from ear to ear. "Are you ready to go back to work?"

Juan wiped himself off with the sheet on the bed before getting himself together. "Actually, I would rather spend the rest of the day locked in this room with you."

"Aww, you're so sweet. But we got to get back to the job," she replied.

They kissed before leaving out of the room. Juan dropped the key off at the front desk and told the clerk he would be back later. In the car, Jennifer resumed implementing her plan.

"Juan, you promised that you would do anything for me. Remember?" she said with a look of concern written all over her face.

"And I meant it, Jenn. What's going on? What do you need for me to do?" Juan replied.

Jennifer explained to Juan what she wanted him to do and why she needed it done. Juan realized he had bit off more than he could chew, but he'd already given his word. He took pride in keeping his word. Not that he was a new jack to the game.

Juan Santiago grew up a Latin King. He'd seen and been a part of more murders than he could account for. More than he'd seen and done since starting at the agency. "No pressure, Jenn. I got you."

Chapter Five

Sun, Moon, Yishi, Yuri, Shyan, and Qi were on their flight. Everyone was caught up in their own thoughts for the most part. Everyone except Yuri and Qi Dom Po. They were fascinated with the fact of visiting America for the first time.

"Would you two stop planning an illusion? This isn't a vacation," Yishi said in a harsh tone.

Yuri kept quiet. He knew talking back to Yishi was a slippery slope. You never know what her reaction was going to be until it came. Qi Dom Po, on the other hand, had not quite figured that much out.

"Master Yishi, I do not see anything wrong with having a little fun while we are in America," Qi said, and before he knew it, he was wiping blood from his bottom lip. Yishi had jumped out of her seat and punched him just that fast.

Shyan shook her head with pity. "Young Master Yishi Pe Sune, spare the ignorant. It is his first journey of the sort. But after this one, he'll understand the importance of staying focus on the objective."

Yishi returned to her seat. "Master Shyan Sune, I hope you're right. I would hate having to discipline Yuri because of such undisciplined influence," she said before her turning on her iPod and relaxing to the sounds of a Chinese version of Sade.

Qi Dom Po looked at Shyan and mouthed thank you so much. She nonchalantly shrugged her shoulders before resting her head on Sun's shoulder. She closed her eyes, allowing the rhythm of her husband's heartbeat and breathing to put her to sleep. Sun looked at Qi and smiled, giving him the thumbs up.

Moon watched the scene from her seat next to a window. She was in deep thought. She wanted to go against everything

Shyan and Sia said. In her mind, Jennifer could've been dead by now and everyone could resume enjoying their lives because she was definitely enjoying hers.

Thinking about the situation in such a manner caused her to wonder what Sia was doing. *'Thinking about me probably,'* Moon thought. She checked the time, it was 11:07 a.m. by her phone, meaning, it was 9:07 a.m. where Sia was.

The thought of going to her lover in spirit crossed her mind, but Moon knew she was not disciplined enough to control the emotions that would come with doing so. So, she dismissed the thought. However, she made a mental note to make sure they explored intimacy on such a high frequency upon her return. The thought alone put a smile upon her face.

Moon changed the playlist on her iPhone. As *Bria Valentina's Here I Cum For You* came through her earbuds, she closed her eyes and enjoyed the images of her and her lover that flowed through her mind.

***

Ma Sune woke up to kisses from her lover. Her body was relaxed from the pleasure given by Zhia. It was nothing below majestic in her mind.

"Good morning, lover," Zhia said.

Ma sat up straight in bed, she yawned and stretched. "Good morning to you too. What time is it?"

"Time for us to make love in the shower before going our separate ways for this sun," Zhia replied.

That's exactly what they did. Zhia and Ma explored each other's bodies with the gentlest touch and passionate kisses. Afterward, Ma Sune made the drive back to her home. It was very satisfying having Zhia as a lover, but she knew it was not going to last forever because of the age difference.

That thought and being alone, she allowed herself to have an emotional moment. It felt good releasing the built-up frustration. She looked in the rearview mirror amazed at the difference made just by allowing her facial expression to change to fit the emotions she was feeling. *'Maybe we will stay lovers,'* she thought.

The show of one emotion brought on several others. Ma Sune began thinking about her daughter Yishi Pe Sune. Her daughter never had the chance to meet her father. The reason being was, Ma Sune had killed him the same night her daughter was conceived.

There she was, Ma Sune, at age 17. Young, intelligent, a fierce warrior and still in possession of her flower. She had been invited to dinner by her boyfriend Shang Di Ming, who's family was one of the wealthiest families of their time. Ma's mother and father agreed to her going under the condition that she be home before midnight.

Shang picked her up in his family's limousine. Instead of it being a dinner, they end up at a house party. Ma Sune did not feel uneasy because she knew almost everyone at the party. The majority of them graduated with her.

She and her boyfriend danced, talked and laughed the night away. Shang offered her a drink, but she declined, stating she do not drink alcohol fused beverages.

"How about a pop then?" he'd asked her. To which she replied, was fine. He walked off and came back ten minutes later carrying a 20-ounce Ginger Ale. It was ice cold and soothing.

Twenty minutes after drinking the Ginger Ale, Ma Sune started to feel dizzy. Everything became a blur. The last thing she saw clearly was her boyfriend's devilish grin. She knew then he had poisoned her drink with a sedative.

When she regained consciousness, they were in the back of the limousine, she was naked, and he was on top of her inside of her, grunting and moaning as he released. Her body felt sore and violated, so she knew he'd raped her repeatedly. How many times was unknown.

"Get off me!" Ma Sune yelled as she fought him off.

Shang, feeling satisfied, did as she demanded. He zipped up his pants and refastened the belt before opening the rear passenger side door. "Get out you slut. I do not ever want to see your face again," he said coldly.

Ma Sune was about to get out, but the thought of being raped nagged at her. She noticed her clothes on the floorboard. While getting dressed she planned her next move. Confident in pulling it off, she smiled inside.

"Shang, I'm not mad at you. I like you as my boyfriend. If you desired my flower, all you had to do is ask," she said assuring.

Shang sighed. "Close the door, let me take you home."

"I need some fresh air, my love. Come. It is a blood moon. Let's take in its energy," she replied. Ma Sune grabbed Shang by the hand, pulling him out of the limousine behind her. She used her peripheral vision to see if they were alone.

"It is a blood moon," Shang said while staring into the heavens.

Ma Sune did not reply. She was studying her surroundings. They were in a forested area. Obviously far away from the city. "This is a beautiful place. Where are we?"

"A couple of miles out of the city," he replied without taking his eyes off the moon.

He'd provided her with all the information she needed to know her way home. "Shang Di Ming, there's a penalty to pay for deflowering the innocent by force."

Before he could redirect his gaze, Ma Sune struck him with the death touch. His eyes locked in the death stare and the gurgling sound made by one drowning inside on their own blood could be heard clearly. As he fell, she struck him again. But this time with a side heel kick to the chest, sending his already lifeless corpse hard to the forest floor.

Ma Sune towered over her rapist. Within his eyes, she could see the reflection of the blood-red moon. At that moment, she vowed to never be with another man. Thankfully, she had learned how to drive.

Ma Sune jumped behind the wheel of the limousine and drove home. When she got there, she did not hesitate to tell her mother and father what had happened. Mae Za Sune and Rashi El Sune listened with a calmness that could not be defined. After hearing the whole story, her parents hugged her and left the compound without saying a word to anyone.

Days later, the news report was printed. The entire Mirg family was found slaughtered beyond recognition. The place they were found was the same place she had been raped and where she had killed her rapist. Nobody was ever called in for questioning or arrested behind it, which was not uncommon when the authorities concluded it was the work of the High Council.

As she exited memory lane, Ma Sune found herself swerving back in the right lane. "Emotions can get you accidentally killed", she thought out loud. She calmed herself emotionally before making it home. Once back within her comfort zone, she was ready to deal with the business calls that she knew awaited her.

Willie Slaughter

Chapter Six

Trent had been laying low. It donned on him Sun nor Shyan had returned his call. That could only mean one thing in his mind. They were on their way to Jersey.

Being that he did not want to be seen walking around, he'd sent Miranda to the ATM to make a withdrawal out of one of his accounts. He also provided her with his clothes and shoe size so she could do some shopping for him. He demanded that she get herself whatever she wanted and whatever she thought he would like to see her in.

While waiting on her to return, he prepared dinner. Afterward, he decided to call Sun again. The line did not make it through a full ring before he answered.

"I got your message. What's good, bro?" Sun said.

"Yeah, shit is real. Someone torched my crib. Anyway, it is all good, bro. What you up to? Where's sis?" Trent replied.

"We are on our way to you. Stay low. It is that broad Jennifer? She is out for revenge," Sun said.

Trent chuckled. "Dammit, man. What did your cousin do to her?"

Sun could not help but laugh, knowing what his friend was referring to. "Aye, that's above my pay grade, bro. My only concern is making sure the devil gets exactly what she is asking for."

"Word, bro," Trent replied. He heard the front door open and Miranda calling him to help with the bags. "Listen, bro, I gotta go."

"Who is that in the background?" asked Sun.

"Just chill. You'll get to know her soon enough. Anyway, I appreciate the info about Jennifer. Now I know what I'm dealing with," Trent responded.

"What we are dealing with, bro. We been in the air for a while, so we will be touching down soon. If you need any more info on her, tap in with Master Diablo," Sun stated.

"Bet. See you when you get here. One," Trent said before hanging up the phone. He hurried out of the kitchen and into the living room to help Miranda. "Apologize for the delay, queen. I was on the phone with my bro. He and his wife are on their way to Jersey."

Miranda did not respond right away. She was still having trouble wrapping her mind around the digits she saw pop up in his account. "That's what's up. An early family reunion, Trent?"

By the look on her face, he knew she had questions. "What's on your mental?"

"Exactly what is it you do for a living?" she asked.

"Why you ask?" he replied.

"You're a multimillionaire and you're living in the hood, Trent. It doesn't make any sense," she responded.

Trent shrugged his shoulders, smiling. "Did not want to leave my neighborhood. Not to mention, I did not want to miss out on this opportunity." Trent relieved her of the bags and tossed them over on the couch before kissing her softly on the lips.

"I've prepared dinner already. Let's eat," he said, leading her by the hand into the kitchen. He seated her at the dining table and proceeded to serve her the stir-fried Wild Alaskan Salmon, sea moss, brown rice, herbs, and spices, over which he poured a gravy made from scratch with raw honey. On the side dish was steamed asparagus smothered in melted vegan butter and nondairy cheese. He served hot mint tea to wash it down.

"Bona petite," he said as he sat in the chair directly across from her.

Miranda ate and drank her share without saying a word.

"So, what you think? Am I qualified to be your chef?" asked Trent.

Not wanting to show bad table manners by talking with a mouth filled with food, Miranda nodded and signaled with a thumbs up. She finished eating and drinking and relaxed in the chair. "That's what I call a meal fit for a queen," she stated while rubbing her stomach.

"Thanks for the compliment, luv," he replied while getting up from the table. He started gathering the dirty dishes. Miranda watched him work for a little while before excusing herself, saying she was going to take a bath and lay it down. "Okay, queen, I'll be on shortly to give you a massage before you fall asleep," Trent said.

Miranda stopped dead in her tracks and turned around. "Poppy, do not start something you cannot keep up."

"As long as you do not ask me to buy you a mansion and all the extra shit, I do not have a problem keeping up everything else. I enjoy simple living," he said without taking his eyes off the task before him.

Miranda did not respond. She just smiled and walked off. She turned on the water in the tub and added coconut-scented bubble bath. She sat on the side of the tub in deep thought while the steaming water filled the tub with bubbles and the air with the coconut fragrance.

'What a great man. He cooks, cleans and takes care of his business,' she thought.

Miranda turned the water off. She relieved her body of its garments and eased herself into the steamy bubble bath. The hot water was comforting to her overworked body. Although she never lagged behind on any bills, it was a struggle. She usually took any overtime she could get and on weekends, she worked Uber Eats, a mobile food escort service. It paid by delivery.

The aroma of the bubble bath caused Miranda to relax mentally. She closed her eyes and enjoyed the miracles the hot bath was working on her. She did not realize she'd dozed off until hearing Trent's voice.

"Someone's real relaxed," he said.

Miranda opened her eyes to stare into his. She did not see the mirrors to his soul. They had a calm and calculating sense about them. "You caught me sleeping, Poppy. How long you been sitting there?"

Trent did not respond right away. He grabbed the sponge and began bathing her. "Long enough to figure out exactly what I'm going to do to your body tonight."

"And what's that, Poppy?" she asked.

He did not say anything. He continued to wash her body. Afterward, he picked her up out of the tub and stood her on her feet. He picked a drying towel from the rack of towels and wrapped it around her wet body before picking her up again and carrying her into the bedroom.

"What's good, Poppy? Why you all silent about everything?" asked Miranda as he laid her down on the queen-size bed.

Trent took a step back and looked at the perfect physique lying on the bed naked before him. "I'm going to put you back to sleep. So, relax and let me have control of this body sexy lady."

"I'm your world, Poppy. Do what you do," she replied.

Trent commenced in being her personal chiropractor. As he realigned her body, Miranda sighed and moaned throughout the process. Then he proceeded to give her a full body massage.

"Poppy, you definitely know how to please your queen," she said in between moans. Instead of feeling a need to sleep, Miranda's sexual appetite became aroused.

Trent continued to massage the soft brown skin. Once he felt satisfied, he stopped and laid on his back next to her. "Mission accomplished," he said with a sigh.

Miranda rolled over on top and straddled him. "Partially." She kissed him passionately on the lips while grinding her sex against him.

"This would work a lot easier if we were both naked. Do not you think?" Trent said.

She kissed him again. "Uh-huh," she replied and got up.

Trent got up out of bed. He undressed standing before her. As the last piece of clothing hit the floor at the foot of the bed, Miranda's lips and hands began exploring his body. Enjoying the touch, he could not help sighing.

"Let's see if we can put each other to sleep, Poppy," she said before pushing down on the bed and climbing back on top. She slid down the length of his erection and let out a moan. "Poppy, you're touching my soul."

Miranda sat still for a moment, allowing herself to adjust to the feeling of him inside of her. Trent was not upset at all. He was enjoying the moment. Her tightness and wetness had him on edge of a pre-release.

Miranda leaned close to him, her breasts pressing against his chest as she kissed him hungrily. She began gyrating her hips slowly. The relaxer her sex became to the feel of his erection, the more she picked up the pace. Before Trent knew it, he was in for the ride of his life.

"Poppy! Poppy!" she yelled while riding the length of his shaft hard and fast. The sound of her soft flesh smacking against his thighs was driving him crazy. But what really had his toes curling was the sloppy wet sound of her sex around his erection.

Trent smacked her on the hips playfully. "Yeah, Mommy, just like that. Yeah, baby. Do not stop Mommy."

Miranda went in overdrive. She rose to the tip of his erection and worked her hips real fast. Feeling himself about to explode, Trent grabbed hold of her waist and thrust up inside of her hard and fast.

"Cum for Mommy, Poppy! Cum for me!" she yelled as her own orgasm flowed. Her body trembled and her lips quivered with every kiss she placed on his lips.

Trent's release came forcefully. He let out a moan of pure pleasure as he filled her up with his release. She slow-grinded until she milked him dry before rolling off the top and resting her head on his chest.

"Goodnight, Poppy," Miranda said as she closed her eyes.

Trent wrapped his left arm around her and kissed her on the forehead. "Great night, luv." He lay listening to her breathing slowed before he closed his eyes and joined her in resting.

The following morning, they awakened to the sound of knocking at the front door. Trent slid out from under Miranda as smoothly as possible. He quickly put on some clothes. Without making any noise, he crept from the bedroom closing the door behind him.

The knocking continued as he made his way to the door. "I'm coming!" He opened the door and smiled. It was Sun, Moon, Shyan, Yishi, Yuri, and Qi. Trent and Sun shook hands and hugged. "Master Sun, I'm so glad to see y'all."

"Likewise, brother," Sun replied.

"Enough with the formalities. It is cold out here," Shyan stated.

"Oh, yeah, sis come in. Make yourselves at home," Trent said stepping aside to let them in. They walked in and Trent showed them into the living room. "Have a seat. Can I get you anything?"

Everyone sat down except Yishi. She walked around the living room looking at the pictures that aligned the walls. "Nice home you have here, Master Trent. Lovely wife," she said stopping in front of a full-body portrait of Miranda.

Trent laughed. "Thanks for the compliment, but she is not my wife yet. We are working on that part."

Yishi nodded still staring at the picture. "I see. Well, some hot tea would be nice Master Trent."

"Okay. Could you give me a moment to get myself together? Y'all did wake me up," Trent replied.

Everybody nodded to show their understanding. Trent walked out of the living room and went back into the bedroom. "Miranda? Queen, wake up."

Miranda's eyelids fluttered open. She sat up in bed and yawned. "Yes, Poppy, I'm awake. What time is it?"

"Seven twenty-five. Why what's up?" he asked.

She got up out of bed and stretched. Looking at her nude body aroused him. He knew in order for him not to take her into his arms and make love to her he had to turn his head.

"I got to get ready for work. You joining me in the shower, Poppy?" she replied while walking towards the bathroom. He stripped out of his clothes and followed her into the shower.

They bathed each other, showered each other with kisses, and made love under the steaming hot water. Afterward, while getting dressed, it donned on her what he had said when he'd waking her up.

"Baby, did you say we have company?" she asked.

"Yeah, queen, my brothers, and sisters are sitting in the living room as we speak. I supposed to be making them some hot tea," Trent replied.

"How did they know where to find you?" she questioned further.

Trent chuckled. "Mommy, we can be on the opposite side of the globe, and still know where to find each other. Do not worry, you're going to see how we operate real soon."

Trent and Miranda finished getting dressed and went into the living room, where their guests awaited their arrival. At first sight, the different shades of brown skin complexions took Miranda by surprise. When Trent had said his brothers and sisters, she had a preconceived image in her mind of what they looked like.

"Miranda, meet my family. This is Masters' Sun, Shyan, Moon, and Yishi. These other two are, Young Masters Qi and Yuri. Everyone, meet Miranda, my wife to be," Trent said.

Yishi, Yuri, Shyan, and Qi bowed. Sun and Moon exchanged hugs with Miranda, who welcomed their affectionate embraces.

"Nice to meet you guys. Unfortunately, I have to go to work. However, when I get off, we can all go out to dinner or we can dine in," Miranda said. She made an attempt to step pass Yuri, but Yishi commanded him to stop her.

"Miranda, you are of our kindred spirit now. I apologize however, we cannot allow you to walk out of this home without knowing you can protect yourself," Yishi stated.

"I appreciate it, Master Yishi, but I can handle whatever comes my way," Miranda said defensively.

"Can you? Well, let's see. Yuri?" Yishi said.

Yuri bowed towards Miranda before getting in his fighting stance. "Sister Miranda, prepare to defend yourself."

Miranda looked at the young Asian boy and smiled. "Yuri, how old are you?"

"I'm eleven, but do not let my age trick you. Now, prepare to defend yourself," he said again, This time more thoroughly.

Miranda put her guard up. "Alright. Let me see what you got." She tried to steal off on Yuri, who swiftly sidestepped the right jab and pushed her off balance. She regained her balance and looked directly at Trent. All he could do was gesture for her to keep her eyes on what was before her.

She went at Yuri with all she had, throwing jab combinations, which everyone found admirable, but not good enough to let her leave the house. Yuri continued to block, sidestep and even counterattacked a couple of times. They continued until Miranda could not swing anymore and had to stop to catch her breath.

"Okay, Young Master Yuri, that's enough. I do believe Sister Miranda understands now," Yishi said.

Yuri, not even breathing hard, stood still and bowed towards Miranda. "Thank you for the opportunity to improve my skills."

That got a chuckle out of Trent and Sun. Both of them recalled the day they'd decided to spar with the young warrior. He had proved to them that he was every bit of a great Sure Warrior as his elders. They knew they had Yishi to thank for it.

"Again, Miranda, I apologize, but you are not to leave your home without an escort. There are very mean people in this world who are out to do harm to our kindred spirits. People who are almost as good of fighters like Young Master Yuri," Yishi stated.

"Besides sis, your hubby got a bank account larger enough for us all to live off without having to work a day in our life," Shyan retorted.

"Believe me, I know," Miranda replied still trying to catch her breath. She sat on the couch next to Shyan. "Well, since I'm not going to work and Yuri has worn me down, that leaves you to cook for us all, Poppy."

"Poppy?" Sun said with a grin on his face. "Come on, bro. We will tackle the kitchen together. That should give us time to catch up." Sun draped his left arm around Trent's shoulder, and they headed for the kitchen.

"Wait on us," Yuri said and grabbed Qi Dom Po by the wrist. He pulled him to his feet.

"What's going on Yuri?" Sun asked.

Yuri looked around at the faces of Yishi, Shyan, Moon, and Miranda. He leaned close to Sun's right ear, fearing Yishi would hear him if he did not. "I do not think it would be appropriate for us to remain amongst the company of women while the men are in the kitchen. Matter of fact, we will be of great help preparing a lovely meal."

Sun nodded to express his understanding. "Looks like we are going to have a Sune's special all day." Trent, Sun, Yuri, and Qi walked on into the kitchen.

Shyan eyed Miranda curiously. Not that she distrusted her. It was the fact that she was with someone she loved and cared for. "So, Miranda, how long have you been knowing Trent?"

Miranda noticed she was the center of everyone's attention. "I've known him since becoming his next-door neighbor. We talked every time we crossed paths. But for the most part, Poppy never showed interest in me until recently."

"I do not think he never showed interest in you. You're a strong-willed woman, exactly what my brother needs in his life. I think he was only protecting you, himself and his heart," Shyan said.

Looking in her eyes, Miranda could tell she was confident in her perception of things. "What exactly is it your family is into?"

"Let's just say we run some very lucrative, but important businesses," she answered. Seeing Miranda's facial expression, she knew she was not buying it. "What the hell. We are assassins and we have our legitimate businesses as well."

"Thank you for being straight up," Miranda replied.

Moon had been quiet, observing Miranda's body language and the vibration that came from her lips with every word spoken, until Shyan put everything out in the open. "Miranda, I'm Moon Tao Po. Now that you know what we are and do, you have a decision to make."

Miranda looked at her, confused. "I'm not understanding."

"Let's try this in layman terms then. Ain't no bitch in anybody's blood in this family. Not saying you're soft or scared, but you gotta tighten up on your hit game. Our family do not run a protection agency. One Po or Sune can easily take out six to seven assassins from another clan or agency of trained fighters. And so, will you," Moon stated in a serious manner.

"Sister Miranda," Yishi interjected. "What Master Moon Tao Po is saying is, you really do not have a choice in the matter. I do believe you've already made up your mind to be with Master Trent. Am I correct?"

Miranda responded with a nod of her head.

"While we are here tending to our affairs, you shall begin training. Yuri shall be your trainer in using weaponry. Master Moon Tao Po shall train you in hand to hand combat," Yishi stated.

"Okay, I'm good with that," Miranda replied. "Is there anything else I need to know that I've unconsciously signed up for?"

"Funny you asked." Shyan began saying. "You two will be returning to Beijing, China with us. You shall be married according to our family's tradition. This isn't up for discussion."

Meanwhile, in the kitchen, Trent, Sun, Yuri, and Qi were cooking a feast. Yuri and Trent were handling the preparations while Qi and Sun did the timing. It was Yuri's idea for them to bake some Alaskan Wild Salmon, make a crust and pour some raw wild honey over the salmon, topped it off with another layer of crust before adding another layer of salmon and pouring more raw wild honey over it. It became a three-layer Alaskan Wild Salmon Pie.

"Let me find out you're trying to steal my girl, Yuri," Trent said jokingly.

"Why would I do that? Do you not know the penalty is death for making a pass at a kindred spirit's counterpart? I'm not trying to die from a thousand cuts," Yuri replied.

Trent looked at Qi for confirmation of what Yuri stated. When he nodded his head, Trent knew Yuri was not joking. "I did not mean it like that, Yuri. I was really complimenting you on your cooking skills."

Yuri bowed honorably. "Thank you, Master Trent. Next time try to be more literal with your statements. The Sune Clan are literal people. We mean what we say and say what we mean."

"Understandable. Let's finish cooking this fly meal and give the ladies something to be thankful for besides our skills on the battlefield," Trent replied.

While they continued to cook, Yishi stepped in the kitchen. She moved so silently they did not even know she was watching them until she spoke, "Young Master Yuri, I see you've remembered your mother's favorite recipe. This should turn out to be a fine meal," she said in Mandarin.

Yuri, startled, turned around and bowed quickly. "Yes, Master Yishi, us men are showing our cooking proficiency this sun. This sun, we cook. This moon, we do our best to handle our affairs so we can be on our way back home," he replied in their native tongue.

Yishi nodded with a look of approval on her face. "Interesting. What I've come to tell you is, you will be training Miranda in using the bow staff."

Yuri's eyes lit up with surprise. He bowed several times and turned his attention back to his task. Trent, on the other hand, scratched his head out of confusion. He was not fluent in Mandarin, but he knew enough to piece together the gist of Yishi and Yuri's conversation.

"Master Trent, is there something you would like to say?" Yishi asked, seeing the confused look in his eyes.

"If he's training Miranda in weaponry only, who is doing the martial training?" he asked in response to her question.

"Master Moon Tao Po," Yishi answered before walking out of the kitchen.

Trent looked at Sun, who hunched his shoulders. "Aye bro, when it comes to the decisions the women make, I just roll with the punches," Sun said.

Thinking about the things he knew Moon had done, Trent shook his head. "Hopefully, my girl will make it through this. Why Moon?"

"Because Master Yishi knows Master Moon Tao Po isn't going to go soft on Miranda," Qi started saying. He washed his hands and dried them off. "Not that any one of us would have gone soft on her. It is all in perception. Once delving into the esoteric way of ninja, the view of life and death changes for the best of all whom you love. Does it make you more ruthless? Yes."

There was complete silence in the kitchen. The timer on the oven buzzing, letting them know the Alaskan Salmon Pie was done brought them back to reality.

"Well, that's done," Yuri said cheerfully. Everything else they cooked was simple. They steamed some whole grain long rice and added spices. Qi Dom Po made a topping from sea moss and other herbs and spices to go over the rice. Trent kept to his word and made the hot tea from fresh tea leaves.

Sun chopped up fresh bell peppers, onions, garlic, and purple radish, and stir-fried it in vegetable oil along with whole-grain long noodles. By the time his portion of the cooking was complete, Trent, Qi and Yuri's were done as well.

"Alright, Master Chefs, let's set the table. Qi, you can tell the women the morning meal is ready," Sun said.

While they set the table, Qi did as he was asked. He returned with Shyan, Yishi, Moon, and Miranda alongside him. Trent asked for them to be seated while they served the food. Once done, Trent sat beside Miranda.

Sun sat beside his wife, Yuri and Qi filled in the empty seats between Moon and Yishi. They ate in silence. The only noise to be heard was the sound of silver wear clanking against the plates.

"That was delicious," Miranda commented.

"Thank you," Yuri replied. No one else cared to compliment the dish because it was a normal daily meal to them. Miranda got up from the table and began collecting dirty dishes. The rest of the women assisted her.

"You're guests, I'll take care of the dishes," Miranda said. Yishi, Shyan nor Moon paid her any mind. They continued to help. After the dishes were washed and put away, all four women returned to their seats at the dining table.

"Alright, Master Trent, give us the rundown without leaving out any details," Sun demanded.

Trent told them, in detail about the day his flight landed in Jersey. "Then I got this eerie feeling that I was being watched and followed. I brushed it off because this is New Jersey. People watch people."

Sun, Shyan, and Moon nodded, showing they understood where he was coming from.

"Yeah, but it is deeper than rap," Sun said. He filled Trent in on Jennifer's plan to destroy them. The whole while, Trent stared into Moon's eyes. He could see her hatred for Jennifer.

"So, bro, we have to tread lightly," Sun said.

"Excuse me," Moon interjected. "But I'm going to go by the house and get my property while she is at work. And Master Sun, I think we should all go stay at Nana and Granddaddy's house. It is big enough and they'll be glad to see us. Not to mention, they'll be surprised to see you're married."

He was almost ready to object until she reminded him, he had not introduced his wife to them. "I agree. We will head on over and get settled in while you're gone to get whatever. Moon Tao Po, in and out," he stated with the I know what you're thinking look in his eyes.

She nodded. "I got you, cousin," she said before leaving.

Shyan looked her husband in the eyes. "Are you sure that's a good idea?"

"I'll go with her," Yishi interjected. She hurried out of the dining room to catch up with Moon.

"Are we sure that was a good idea?" Yuri asked. Nobody answered because it donned on them what Yuri was really asking. Yuri shook his head. "Death and the Grim Reaper politely excuse themselves, and nobody sees anything wrong with it."

Miranda scratched her head. The child had a way with his words. "Excuse me, Yuri. How old did you say you are again?"

"Alright, let's go," Shyan blurted out, seeing a question about to turn into a lecture on age being pointless. "It is time to go meet the in-laws. Miranda, pack light, please. We will go shopping after settling at Freeman's Estate."

After all, she'd heard and experienced first-hand, Miranda did not ask any questions. She left out followed by Trent. Together, they packed some clothes and cosmetics into backpacks and returned to the kitchen. "We are ready to go," Trent said hefting a backpack on each shoulder.

"Let's ride," Sun replied. They walked out of the house. Shyan and Yuri rode with her husband. Qi rode with Trent and Miranda. Sun led the way in a rental that he planned on returning after everyone met over his grandparents' place.

The drive was longer than they hoped because of rush hour. Pedestrians and corporate workers were on the tare. "Man, we just had to get caught in midday traffic. The main reason I always preferred Amtrak," Sun said.

Shyan rested her head on the headrest and sighed. Yuri could not make sense of what their frustration was about. He sat in the backseat by himself trying to figure out what it was. Realizing it was not adding up in his mind, Yuri tapped the back of Shyan's seat. "I apologize if I'm being annoying at the moment, Master Shyan."

"You're not being annoying yet," she replied.

Yuri took her response as an invitation to speak further. "It seems as if something has caused you and Master Sun to become frustrated. I'm not quite understanding what happened."

Sun, knowing what he was getting at, began laughing. "Chill babes. I got this one," he said to Shyan, who nodded and closed her eyes. "Yuri, have you ever driven a car before?" Sun asked.

"No. I prefer to walk wherever I have to go," Yuri answered.

"And why is that?" Sun asked in response.

"Because my feet can get me in and out of places a car cannot," he replied.

Sun nodded his head. "That's a great reason for not wanting to drive if I've ever heard one. It is pretty much the same reason behind our frustration. We are stuck in a traffic jam, so we are going nowhere fast."

Yuri relaxed on the backseat. "I knew we should have walked."

"Or caught the Amtrak," Shyan inputted.

Traffic continued moving slow. Whether they knew it or not, their minds were on the same thing. What Yishi and Moon were doing at the moment.

Willie Slaughter

Chapter Seven

Yishi and Moon arrived at Jennifer's house. The first thing Moon noticed was. Jennifer's 911 Porsche parked in the driveway.

"Looks like we might have to sneak in," Moon said.

"And why is this?" Yishi asked.

"Because that's Jennifer's work car. If it is parked out front, she is probably in the house," she replied.

"Is it the only means of transportation?" she questioned.

"No," Moon answered. She did not want to believe Jennifer would drive her car to work, but it was the other option of transportation. "Let's check the garage first."

The two women walked around to the two-door garage as if they lived there. Moon knew where the spare key to the side door was kept just in case of an emergency. She opened the lid of George Foreman Grill and grabbed the spare key that was mixed with the unused charcoal. She unlocked the side door, and they stepped inside.

"Your intuition was correct." Moon stated seeing her Audi 8 was not parked inside. She led the way into the house through the door within the garage. Everything looked just as she remembered it.

"Nice place," Yishi complimented. "It is a shame the owner of it has to die soon."

"More like a blessing the owner shall die soon. Right this way," Moon said and walked down the hallway into the master bedroom. She did not even care to look at the bed. Her mind was on getting her gear and weapons and leaving.

While Moon entered the walk-in closet and opened the secret compartment in the back behind the clothes, she found herself in deep thought. She wanted to lay in the shadows until

Jennifer got home and end her life. However, she knew Shyan wouldn't let her live it down, so she shrugged the thought off. All her things were exactly where she'd left them. She smiled and placed her swords, daggers and ninja stars and cleaning solutions inside the duffle bag.

"Master Moon Tao Po, I think you should come see this," Yishi called out from inside the bedroom. Moon grabbed the duffle bag and hurried out of the closet to see what Yishi was talking about. When Yishi turned around holding up the white ninja suit, her eyes widened with surprise.

"Excuse my language. Where in the hell did you find that?" Moon said.

"It was laid out on the bed. Cute do not you think?" Yishi asked as she placed it back on the bed how she found it. "Maybe we need to do some more investigating. It is obvious this devil is more than what she has been letting on to be."

Moon nodded in agreement. "Well, I've retrieved what I came for. We will inform the others of our findings when we meet up with them over my grandparents' place."

"Okay. One last thing before we go." Yishi took out her iPhone and snapped a couple of pictures of the ninja suit on the bed. "Now we have proof of our findings. Let's go."

They left out the same way they'd entered the house. Moon put the spare key back inside the George Foreman Grill. They walked the two blocks to the Amtrak terminal and caught the train. Not liking being crowded, they sat in the seats all the way in the back.

"What are you pondering?" Yishi asked. By Moon's body language and facial expression, since they'd left Miranda's house, Yishi could tell she was considering some options.

"I just want to get this over with as soon as possible. We are here now. Me and Shyan know the city. There's no reason we should prolong our being here," Moon replied.

Yishi nodded. She was thinking the same thing. "I agree with you one hundred percent. I was actually hoping the devil had been home. We could be on our way back home."

That had been Moon's plan all along, but she just kept the thought to herself, seeing her and Yishi shared the view on the matter. They stayed silent the rest of the ride. Not because they did not have anything to say to each other, but more so out of observing their surroundings. They knew it was a possibility they were being spied on.

As they walked across the street towards Moon's grandparent's estate, Yishi nodded approvingly. "This is definitely a more suitable place to rest while we are here."

"Yeah, welcome to mysterious land," Moon replied as they entered through the side gate. She recalled the last time she'd been inside the place. The things her grandmother had shown her. The secrets that rested behind locked doors.

"Yes, most places of the sort hold secrets that are meant to remain secrets," Yishi stated.

Moon rang the doorbell three times. "That you're so right about." Before she could press the button again, Sun opened the door and stepped outside, pulling the door shut behind him.

"Heads up. Remember, this is our grandparent's spot. There's no need in trying to get them to understand who Sun Sune and Moon Tao Po are. Shyan is Angela, you are Tabitha, and I'm Kenneth. Okay?" Sun said.

Both women nodded to show they understood what he was asking of them before he opened the door and they all walked in. Kenneth led them into the den, where everyone was seated listening to his grandmother talk about the estate and a brief history of their family.

"Hey, Granny!" Tabitha screamed and ran over to where she sat and hugged her neck while kissing her on the right cheek. "How have you been?"

Her grandmother hugged her back. "Oh, I've been alright Tabitha. These old bones have not failed me yet. Who is this lovely young lady you have with you?"

Tabitha stood up straight and beckoned for Yishi to come closer. "Grandma, meet my sister Yishi Pe Sune. Yishi Pe Sune, meet my grandma."

"Nice to meet you Yishi Pe Sune," Tabitha's grandmother said.

Yishi bowed out of respect for the elder. "Likewise, Grandma."

"Yo' Tabitha," her grandfather interjected. "You do not know anybody other than your granny? What about, Papa? I need some love, too."

Tabitha hurried over to him. She hugged her grandfather and kiss on the left cheek. "Papa, you know it is nothing but love here." After hugging her grandfather, she and Yishi took a seat.

"I know you young folks are exhausted from your flight, so y'all should go freshen up and get some rest. And Kenneth Freeman, you know where y'all married folks and couples will be sleeping. Only hanky panky going on in the main house is your grandfather and me," his grandmother said.

"Yes ma'am," he replied. "Alright, let me show everyone to their rooms. Every room has its own bathroom and bath, so nobody has to worry about getting lost looking for the bathroom." Kenneth, followed by his wife and the others, left the den. He dropped Yishi, Moon, Yuri, and Qi off at their rooms, which appeared to look the same in décor.

Miranda was astounded. She'd lived and visited nice places, but the prestige of the Freeman's Estate was awing. "So, where will we be sleeping?"

Kenneth smiled. "Right this way." He led them down a long hallway that took them out of the main house into a courtyard. There was a row of small houses like rooms on the other side. "Here's where we will be sleeping."

"Are there particular ones?" Trent asked.

Kenneth shrugged his shoulders. "Pick one. They are all the same." He did not have to say it twice for his wife to understand. Angela walked directly over to the one she'd in her sights since seeing them.

"While you get settled in, I'm going to go get Yishi, Moon, Yuri, and Qi. We can have a meeting in one of the empty sleeping quarters or out in the courtyard. Either is fine here because nobody gets in anybody's business around here." Kenneth said and walked off. He carried his and Angela's bags inside their room before leaving to get the others for the meeting.

Willie Slaughter

Chapter Eight

Jennifer and Juan were having dinner. Juan had made reservations for them at a five-star restaurant in the downtown area not too far from the federal building. Whatever it was she wanted him to do was nagging at his conscience, which was the real reason he planned the dinner date in the first place. They'd asked for the nonsmoker's area and a table near the window.

"This is nice," Jennifer complimented Juan's taste of dining.

Juan signaled for a waitress. After ordering and the waitress left to fulfill their order, his daunting expression turned serious. "Okay, Jenn, let's discuss business. What exactly is it you want me to do? No games. No bullshit. Let's be straight up."

Jennifer's smile faded from her face. *'Now, things are going as planned,'* she thought. "Well, you know of my little investigation I got going on?"

He nodded. "I wouldn't call it little, but yeah. Go on, I'm listening."

"I'm going to need some hired hands for protection and a little extracurricular detailed work. As for you, I just need your eyes and ears inside of the agency," she said.

Juan frowned. "Sounds like you're having trust issues with someone on the inside. What's really going down?"

Jennifer's expression changed from serious to a cold, calm one. "If you're asking me if I trust our superiors, no, I do not. An investigation this big, and he's willing to dismiss it on account of what happened to the other agents who were assigned to the meat locker case. You damn right, I do not trust him or anyone who agrees with him."

Juan shook his head. "I do not know about that one Jenn. Wade is a straight-up guy. He's been nothing but great to my family. So, if you're asking me to distrust a man who has shown me nothing but loyalty, that's not going to happen. I do not have a problem with keeping my eyes and ears open for you, nor with the hired hands. Anything extra is out of my league."

"Let's enjoy dinner. We will finish this conversation in a more appropriate environment," Jennifer replied. Her thoughts were on killing Juan, but she knew his part in her plan was valuable.

They ate dinner, drank some of the finest wines at Juan's expense, and allowed the soft jazz as well as the laughter within the room to set their mood. The woman three tables up from theirs was the loudest. Her date had just proposed to her. Jennifer watched with jealousy in her heart as the man placed the diamond ring on the woman's finger.

"You'll get your chance," Juan stated seeing her all into the proposal scene. What he did not know was, Jennifer was not thinking about being proposed to or marriage. Her jealousy caused her thoughts to become malicious.

"Maybe. Maybe not." She shrugged her shoulders while stating. "Come on." She grabbed Juan by the hand.

"Whoa. Where are we going?" he asked.

"To congratulate the lovebirds," Jennifer replied.

Hand in hand, Jennifer and Juan scrolled over to the couple's table. Both of them put on their award-winning smiles before reaching their destination.

"Hi, my name is Jennifer, and this handsome man here is Juan," she said.

"Nice meeting you. I'm Tabitha, and this is my fiancé Trent," the woman replied.

Hearing the names, Jennifer's jealousy transformed into hatred. It took everything within her to control her body language. "Wow! That's wonderful. I was telling Juan that it appeared you were being proposed to, and I wanted to congratulate you on your new engagement."

"Thanks a lot," Tabitha replied.

Jennifer took out her Galaxy S10. "Do you mind if I get a picture of us together? Something to remember and for motivation because I'm looking forward to getting married one day, but I be needing help to get over the jittery and anxiety that comes with the realization of being a spouse."

"No problem," Trent interjected. He called for one of the waitresses. "Excuse me, ma'am. Would you snap a few photos for us?"

"Sure," the waitress replied. She grabbed Jennifer's phone and waited for them to tell her to start snapping shots. Once Tabitha gave the word, she took ten pictures of the two couples together. "Here you go."

"Thanks," Jennifer said as she grabbed the phone and began looking at the pictures. "What's your phone number?"

Tabitha gave her the number, and she forwarded the ten pictures through multimedia text messages in a slide show format.

"Well, it was nice meeting you, Tabitha and Trent. The night is still young, and you have put me in a mood," Jennifer said with a wink of her right eye at Tabitha.

The dark, chocolate-skinned woman grinned. "I understand girlfriend. Do your thang. You got my number. Hit me up. We will kick it sometimes when I'm not busy."

Jennifer gave her the thumbs up before walking off. Once she and Juan got back to their table, the smiles diminished quickly.

"What was that all about?" Juan asked.

"Juan, I want—better yet, you better fuck me good tonight before we part ways," was Jennifer's reply, which caused Juan to grunt out of surprise.

"Excuse me, waiter," Juan said while waving the young clean shaved man over to their table. "Come on with the bill."

The man smiled and nodded before walking off and returning with the ticket. Juan handed the man his credit card. He swiped it on the handheld electronic device and handed it back to him. "Have a great evening sir."

Juan did not care to respond. The meal had cost him $725, but it got him exactly what he wanted. Another go-round with Jennifer. They walked out of the restaurant into the crisp evening air.

"Where to?" Juan asked as they walked through the parking lot to his car.

"Just drive," Jennifer responded after getting in on the passenger side. "Matter of fact," she began to say while getting out. "I'll drive."

Juan hopped from behind the wheel, letting her have the driver's seat. She drove to a hill outside of the city. By the time they arrived the sky was dark blue. Jennifer turned the lights off and killed the engine before getting out and telling Juan to join her.

Jennifer sat up on the hood of the car, pulled the miniskirt up, and slid her panties off. The hood was warm against her naked flesh. "What are you waiting on, an invitation to do what I've already demanded you to do?"

Juan, already aroused, unbuttoned his pants and pulled his erect penis through the open. He snatched Jennifer by the waist to the edge of the hood and penetrated her, causing her to moan and gasp. Without any kissing involved, he began banging her hard.

"Yes! Fuck me with that big cock baby! Yes!" she screamed while staring into his eyes. Her thoughts were on everything besides what was going on at the moment. She was even having thoughts about killing him after he fulfills his duties.

"So, you like it rough, huh?" Juan asked. He pulled her into every thrust. Feeling himself about to cum, he pulled out and calmed himself. Once the rush left his erection, he snatched Jennifer off the hood of the car, bent her over, and rammed his member inside of her. "You like it rough, baby?"

"Oh, my god! Yes! Yes! Mm—" Jennifer screamed at the top of her lungs. She thrust herself back on to him as hard as he pounded inside of her. When the rush came again, Juan did not attempt to stop the inevitable. He came strong inside of Jennifer.

"I can feel you flowing inside of me," she said, being aware of his release. She grinded against him, milking him dry and enjoying her on orgasm. After her flow stopped, Juan backed up out of her and buttoned up his pants.

"Why Jennifer?" he asked while staring into her eyes.

She straightened up and smoothed down her skirt and kicked her panties aside. She hunched her shoulders with a straight face. "Why what? Why I choose to let you cum inside of me? Why what?"

"Jennifer, I'm falling in love with you. Do not you see it?" Juan replied.

Jennifer did not answer him. Instead, she walked around the car and got in on the passenger side. He jumped behind the wheel and started the engine.

"Are you going to answer me, Jenn?" he pleaded.

"Agent Santiago, live free of love. It is a heartless bitch in my book," she replied. *'Your feelings are the cause of your death,'* she thought.

Chapter Nine

Kenneth had returned with Yuri, Qi, Moon, and Yishi. He'd left them standing out in the courtyard while he went to go get Angela, Miranda, and Trent. When they came outside and huddled in a circle with the others, the decision was made to have the meeting in the courtyard since the weather was fair.

"Brothers and Sisters, there's two ways this matter can be handled. We must conduct our affair here as we would if we were home. So, let's hear the plans, and vote on the best course of action," Kenneth said.

The silence lingered amongst them for a while. It was as if neither wanted to speak of their plans if they had one at all.

"Okay," Tabitha began, "I'll speak my peace first. We are in Jersey now, so it would be nothing for me to do what I do best and get this shit over with."

Everyone remained silent after hearing what she had to say.

"I'm in agreement with M—Tabitha," Yishi started to say. "Matter of fact, if the devil had been home today, we would be on our way back to China already."

"Oh, trust and believe, Master Yishi Pe Sune, we already knew this much," Yuri interjected. "I will not even say it would have been a bad idea."

The silence returned. No one seemed to be in disagreement to Tabitha's plan. "Oh, I almost forgot," Yishi blurted out. She took out her phone. "Check out this." She scrolled through her photos until she came upon those of the white ninja suit. "This is what we stumbled across inside of the devil's lair."

Yishi passed the phone to Angela. After looking at the picture from different angles, she passed it to her husband. Everyone got the opportunity to view the photos of the ninja suit before Yishi got the phone back in her possession.

"Dammit man," Miranda said while laughing. "Please excuse my humor. Ninjas in Jersey? Hell no." She cut the laughter short, realizing no one else found humor in the matter.

"What do you think your hubby is?" Angela asked a little more defensively than intended. "Besides, if we were only up against regular street thugs, you wouldn't need any training."

Miranda gave a silent nod, showing she understood. Trent had been quiet through the meeting. His thoughts were focused more on getting it over with and moving forward in life than how the matter would be taken care of.

"I have a suggestion," Qi Dom Po said. Once everyone gave their undivided attention, he continued, "We can never be too sure that Jennifer has not created allies. So, we need to get rid of her allies first then take care of her. Something I think should be left up to Master Trent to do personally since it is his house she blew up."

Trent nodded his head with a smile on his face. "I like your way of thinking. So, how will we find out who her allies are and who will take them out?"

"If I had to orchestrate the plan, personally, I would have Masters' Moon and Shyan seek out the allies. Their craft is undetectable by people who don't know their craft. When it comes to the actual killing of her allies, I would have Masters' Yishi, Yuri and myself do because we are unknown in this country. Jennifer and those who are closest to her, I would leave up to Masters' Sun, Trent and, if Masters Shyan and Moon desire to assist, them to handle it."

The silence returned, but everybody was nodding their heads in agreement with Qi Dom Po's plan.

"So, are we all in agreement with Qi Dom Po?" Kenneth asked. Everyone gave their consent. "With this settled, let's all get some rest. We will begin our tasks tomorrow. Angela and

Trent, we have extra work to do. However, we will discuss this another time."

They went their separate ways. Tabitha, Yuri, Yishi, and Qi went back inside the main house. Trent and Miranda went back inside their place. Kenneth and his wife found themselves making love inside their homely room, which was a miniature house. It was furnished with all the amenities of a house.

"Mm—Mr. Kenneth Freeman, I can do this with you all night long," Angela said as they climaxed together. She placed kisses all over his neck while grinding slowly on top of him. Feeling his erection return, she bounced up and down the length of his shaft until they both released again.

"Is Mrs. Freeman satisfied now?" Kenneth asked in a teasingly way.

Angela did not respond, she laid down flat on top of him and fell asleep.

"I guess that answers my question," he said before following her lead.

**

Jennifer was back home, the first thing she did was jump in the shower. While showering, she masturbated, thinking about her moment with her new flame Tatiana. Afterward, she dried off while standing before the full body mirror in the bedroom.

"Sexy me," she said, standing with her hands on her hips. Jennifer looked at the wall clock. It was 10:26 p.m. "Time to ruin a future."

Jennifer put on the white ninja suit. She walked out of her bedroom over into the computer room and turned on the high-tech computer system. She typed Tabitha's phone number and launched the search engine. While she waited for the data, she was looking for to pull up, she kicked her feet up on the desk and relaxed.

The search engine completed the search command Jennifer typed. Tabitha's information popped up on the screen. Her name, date of birth, SSN, residence and picture ID. Jennifer's only interests were in the picture and residence.

Everything else did not matter. *'And will not matter after tonight,'* she thought. She sent herself an e-mail of the info on Tabitha, so it would be on her phone. Having the easy part of her mission done, she shut down the computer system and walked back inside the bedroom.

Jennifer stepped inside the walk-in closet. She opened the secret compartment that her ex-lover would never think she knew existed. But as Jennifer looked inside, her eyes widened with fear. The swords, daggers, and stars she sought were gone.

"That can only mean one thing," she thought out loud. Jennifer walked back into the bedroom. "That's why you always plan ahead," she said to herself as she got down on her knees on the right side of the bed.

She pulled a rectangular case from beneath the bed, sat it on the bed, and opened it. Inside were her own personal sword, daggers and ninja stars she had ordered. She attached the weapons in a way that each one would be easily accessible when or if needed. Once she was done, Jennifer stood in front of the full-body mirror to inspect herself. She grinned devilishly behind the mask. Now that she knew her ex-lover was back in town, she was motivated to fulfill her bloodlust this night.

Jennifer left out through the garage. Not wanting to risk being seen by a neighbor. Again, she decided to drive her ex-lover's car. As she drove, the feeling of another presence in the car came over her. Jennifer adjusted the rearview mirror to see the backseat better. There was no one there.

'Hold it together, Jenn,' she thought, shaking the feeling off.

She turned on the GPS, typed in Tabitha's address and, once the route to her house popped up on the screen, she magnetized the iPhone to the dashboard. Right after Jennifer posted her phone, she felt a light breeze whirl around inside the car. The windows were up, and the air conditioner wasn't on, so it brought about an eerie feeling.

"Ghosts," she said out loud.

Little did she know, Moon had been present the whole time.

Moon traveled light speed to the destination she'd read off Jennifer's GPS. She was determined to make sure Jennifer's plans were spoiled. When she reached the address, Moon realized the couple was already settled in for the night. As she walked through the walls, she contemplated how she was going to save their lives. One thing she knew for sure was she had to wake them up.

Moon seeped through the bedroom wall and stood over the peacefully resting man and woman. Moon surveyed the room to find something useful that she could knock down to cause one or both of them to wake up. The only thing she saw that seemed plausible was the alarm clock on the man's side of the bed. She concentrated all her energy on pushing the button on the alarm clock to trigger the alarm, and it was a success.

The buzzer alarm sounded off within the bedroom. The man rolled over and blindly reached for the alarm clock to turn it off. After trying twice and not hitting the right button, the woman woke up.

"Trent, what time did you set the alarm for?" she asked while yawning.

Finally, he hit the right button. "I set it for 5:45 a.m. like you asked me to, Tabitha."

When the man called her name, Moon flinched. Now she knew why Jennifer was so bent on killing the couple. It was their names, Trent and Tabitha. Although she did not want to do it, Moon knew what she had to do in order to save the couple.

Without hesitation, she made herself visible to them. Tabitha gasped for air and tapped her fiancé on the arm. "Trent, there's a spirit standing at the foot of our bed."

He rolled over, seeing the brightly glowing humanoid form at the foot of the bed, he sat straight up. "Oh, my God!"

Moon held an illuminance finger to her lips to silence them before she spoke. "Calm down, I'm not here to cause you harm," Moon said calmly.

"Well, what do you want?" asked Trent.

"Listen, you do not have much time. Your lives are in danger," she replied.

"Why would anyone want to hurt us?" Tabitha asked.

"No time to answer all of your questions. Get up, get dressed, and follow me. Your lives depend on your cooperation," Moon answered.

Trent and Tabitha got up out of bed in a hurry. Both of them were spiritually inclined, so they took messages from spirits seriously. Once dressed, Trent grabbed his car keys. "Where to?"

"Are you familiar with New Jersey?" she asked. They nodded. "You're going to The Freeman's Estate. Do you know where this is located?" Moon said.

Trent nodded. "Yes, I know the place."

"Good, hurry. Time is very essential to your livelihood. The woman who seeks to kill you is on her way to your home now,"

Moon said. She stayed close to Trent and Tabitha as they walked out to their car. Once safely inside and en route, Moon traveled back to her physical body and opened her eyes.

She sat up in bed and got herself together before getting out of bed. Out of bed, she walked out of the house and went to stand at the gated entrance, waiting on the couple's arrival. She could not help but smile inside and on the surface.

'You won't have it your way Jennifer,' she thought, seeing the headlights approaching.

The car pulled to a stop at the gates. The driver's side window slid down, revealing Trent's identity. "Excuse me, ma'am. I'm—"

"You're Trent, and your companion is Tabitha. Come on inside, I've been expecting you," Moon said, cutting him off.

Trent drove through the gates and stopped and waited on further instructions once she opened them. Moon opened the rear passenger door and hopped in. "My name is Tabitha Greene."

The other Tabitha scratched her head. She was a little confused. But one thing she was not confused concerning was the sound of her voice. "Why does your voice sound so familiar?"

"Trent, drive on around the bend. You're going to park around back," Tabitha said, avoiding answering the question.

After they parked, Tabitha led them through the main house, out into the courtyard and settled them inside the room between Kenneth and Trent's rooms.

"Do you have a security camera system installed at your house that's accessible by your phone?" Tabitha asked the couple.

"Yes, we do," answered Trent. He took out his cellphone and pulled up the footage of every camera. "Here you go." He handed her the phone.

"Now, to show you what's going on inside of your house, right now," Tabitha said. She observed the movement on the cameras outside and inside. "There." She spotted the blur of the white ninja suit. Actually, she found it surprising that Jennifer moved so swiftly.

Trent and his fiancé Tabitha watched the figure dressed in all white creep into their bedroom. Without hesitating or getting a clear view of the bed, the figure unsheathed a sword and began stabbing the bed repeatedly.

"Damn," Tabitha said. "Whoever that is, definitely wanted us dead. But why?" She turned her questioning gaze to their host.

"Her name is Jennifer. She is a psychopathic bitch who has a serious vendetta against my family. Just so happens, you and your man share names with two of us. I'm Tabitha Greene as I've said earlier, and my brother's name is Trent," she replied.

"Jennifer. Jennifer. Why does the name ring a bell?" Tabitha contemplated.

"Was not that the name of the woman in the restaurant who took pictures with us?" her fiancé asked.

She nodded in deep thought. "Yup, damn sure was. Matter of fact, I still have the pictures saved on my phone." Tabitha pulled out her iPhone 11 and pulled up her photos. "Is that the crazy bitch stabbing an empty bed?"

Tabitha looked at the photos and nodded her head. "That's her." It donned on her who the guy in the picture was. "Well, I'll be a fucking monkey's uncle. Agent Juan Santiago."

"You called him out," Trent confirmed.

Silence filled the air while they continued to watch the footage of Jennifer creeping through the house, stabbing every bed in every bedroom. Trent shook his head in disbelief and said, "I knew something was off about them two."

Tabitha was a little tickled by seeing Jennifer in the white ninja suit stabbing the empty beds. "Alright, it's been a long night for all of us. In the morning, I'll be around to wake you up and introduce y'all to the fam," she said while yawning. Her activity had gotten the best of her.

"What about our jobs? We are working on building our future," Trent said.

"You'll be alright. As long as you abide by our family's rules, all of your needs will be met. Not to mention, you'll be back in your own house soon," Tabitha replied and walked out, closing the door behind her. Out in the courtyard she looked up in the starry sky. It was a Waxing Moon. She stood motionless, thinking about Sia while staring at the moon.

"Aren't you out late young lady?" the voice of her grandmother came behind her. Tabitha continued to stare at the moon. She walked on over and stood beside her granddaughter. "Yes, it is a beautiful night out. It's been a while since I've enjoyed such peace and quietness."

"It is definitely needed," Tabitha replied.

Her grandmother faced her, looking into her granddaughter's eyes, she could see the weariness. "Child go get you some rest. If you're not up early, I'll make sure the people get fed. However, I'm going to let you introduce them to everybody."

Tabitha hugged her grandmother. "Thanks, Nana. I'll see you in the morning," she said and went about her way. As soon as her head touched the soft feather made bed and pillows, she was out like a light.

Willie Slaughter

Chapter Ten

Sia and Saki sat side by side at the opposite end of the table of Ma Sune and Zhia. In between the four, seated around the table, were masters of other clans. It was Ma Sune's vision of a new High Council. Everyone sat quietly, waiting on Ma Sune to begin the meeting.

Finally, she stood to her feet and bowed to everyone. "Greetings kindred spirits. Welcome to our first official High Council meeting. I am honored to stand before you all this sun. No, I'm not the head of this High Council. We are all the head, body and tail of it—" She paused to let the meaning of her statement settle in their consciousness. "Now, I will let Master Zhia Yang have her say," Ma Sune said and sat back down.

Zhia stood and bowed. "Thank you, Master Ma Sune. As some of you know, there's been much trouble concerning human cargo. What do I mean when I say human cargo? Some clans delight in child slavery and things of a distasteful sort. I'm here to tell you there's no place for anyone to hide who chooses to deal in such crimes. They will be hunted down and face the same penalty of death that others have faced in the past and recently. In other words, kindred spirits, let's keep all businesses pure of illegal activities," Zhia demanded.

Lin Su Wen of the Wen Clan raised her hand. Zhia already knew what she wanted to ask because it was well known that the Wen Clan dealt in the drug trade. They ran China's largest underground drug distribution route.

"Speak your peace, Master Lin Su Wen," Zhia said, acknowledging her upraised hand.

Lin let her armrest on the top of the table. "The children and all other forms of enslavement is understood. The Wen Clan disagrees with it just as much as Sune, Po and Yang Clans. But, what about the drug trade? Does this fit into your description of illegal activities that aren't prohibited?"

Zhia shrugged her shoulders. "That depends on how you choose to smuggle them. If it comes through my shipping company and is detected, you will not be receiving your shipment, nor will the buyer it is being shipped to."

Lin nodded. "Fair enough."

"And that's all I can ask of any of you, including myself. Let's understand each other to prevent further bloodshed," Zhia said, ending her speech and sitting back in her chair at the right hand of Ma Sune.

One after the other, the masters and representatives from each clan stood and spoke. Expectations were thrown about the room in a respectful manner. Some of them everybody agreed to uphold. Then there were some several of the members disagreed on that the elders who were present called for a vote to settle the disagreement.

Once they knew where each other stood, refreshments were brought out and they took to casual conversing about business. Sia sat quiet, observing the body language of those who were not Po, Sune or Yang. Although she was studying them, her main focus was on Moon. She knew everything was alright, but she desired to have her at her side and in her bed.

"Cousin, I would rather be in Jersey with them, too," Saki said as if reading Sia's thoughts.

Sia responded with a nod of the head. She did not want to break her concentration at the moment. Between reading the energy coming from their guests and dealing with her own emotions, it made a perfect blend. She found the ability to handle both simultaneously interesting.

"If you're thinking about her that much. Why don't you call her?" Saki asked.

"Because I know she wouldn't want me to," Sia replied. "Excuse me," she said to get everyone's attention. "Is this meeting over? I have other business that demands my attention."

"Of course, Master Sia Po, this meeting is over," Ma Sune answered.

Sia and Saki stood, bowed, and left together. Saki was just as ready to leave as Sia was. The two masters stood out, enjoying the early morning sun rays for a moment before getting in their separate rides and leaving.

Ma Sune and Zhia waited to be the last ones. Once they knew they were alone, Zhia locked the door and ran into Ma's embrace, kissing all over her face while removing her clothes. "I've been waiting all night for this moment."

Ma Sune tried to undress Zhia, but she wouldn't allow her to. "No, lover. I want to taste you," Zhia said before helping Ma Sune lay down on top of the table and kissed her way down to Ma's sex.

"O Zhia," Ma Sune moaned as she licked and sucked on her clitoris. The sensational feeling of her moist tongue and lips against the softness of her flesh caused Ma's body to move with its motion.

Zhia continued to fulfill her hunger for Ma. As Ma Sune's legs locked around her shoulders and began to tremble, Zhia thrust her tongue deep inside of her sex, causing Ma to reach and go beyond her peak of ecstasy. Her sweet tasting fluids flowed over Zhia's tongue.

"Mmm—now I'm full, lover," Zhia said as she stood up straight and wiped her mouth with the back of her hand. Ma Sune, overwhelmed with pleasure, lay, breathing sporadically for a while before getting herself together.

"So, my love, what do you think so far about our version of a High Council?" Ma asked.

Zhia shrugged her shoulders. "I do not know. It seems to be a step in the right direction, but Master Lin Su Wen might become a menace."

Ma Sune nodded in agreement. She had sensed the negative energy of Lin Su Wen before she left the meeting. "Master Lin Su Wen's blood isn't exempt from staining the blade of my sword."

"I do concur," Zhia replied.

After Ma Sune was done getting back dressed, the two women left the meeting place. Zhia jumped on her gold and black tiger stripe Kawasaki Ninja and sped off. She had to get to the docks and signature documents before anything could be imported or exported.

Ma Sune drove her 500 Benz in the same direction as Zhia, but she turned off on the first exit. She had her fabric business to tend to. Thinking about the work at the office, she thought about the sweatshop and took a left turn onto a back road. It led her right to the street where the sweatshop compound was located.

Ma Sune pulled up to the gate. The guards at the outpost knew who she was without having to visually see her because of the green mantis emblem she had put in the place of the Mercedes symbol. Since taking over the compound by force and death, Ma Sune and Zhia had posted the flags of their clans at the entrance. They done so to show ownership of the property and business, moreover, to protect those who worked and lived there.

"Master Ma Sune," one of the guards walked over to the driver's side window and said. "There has been a little trouble. The Lee Clan has attempted to take back the compound."

Her anger flared within, but not on the surface, "So, what happened?"

"They attacked right after shift change. Most of them found death by the edge of our swords, some retreated, and we captured a few. They are being kept in the woods behind the main office," he replied.

Ma Sune nodded and drove through the open gates. She made a beeline to the location the guard had given. After parking in front of the main office, she hurried around back and into the woods. She found herself on a dirt trail, leading Southward, and about forty feet in front of her, she saw a Green Mantis and Golden Tiger holding three hostages at sword point.

Ma Sune hurried over and began her interrogation. She asked the assassins question after question in Mandarin. Neither responded. They held to their silence.

She found it unusual for one of the Grey Rhinos to have so much discipline, so Ma Sune ordered that their shirts be stripped off. Without hesitation, the Green Mantis and Golden Tiger tore the shirts from the captives' bodies. Just as she had suspected, they were not Grey Rhino. They were of the Wen Clan.

"If you value the lives of your kindred spirits, you will tell me what I want to know," Ma Sune said in Mandarin. She knew their lives did not mean anything to them. If it did, they wouldn't have tried to attack a compound protected by Sune and Yang Clans. But she knew they did value the lives of their family.

"We acted independently with the Lee Clan after Master Lin Su Wen told us how you are cutting off our trade route," one of the assassins replied in Chinese.

"You say, you acted independently, but did Master Lin Su Wen order you not to do anything of the sort?" she asked.

97

"No, Master Ma Sune, she did not," he answered.

Ma Sune shook her head with pity. She instructed the Green Mantis and Golden Tiger to stand down and give them some space. They sheathed their swords and backed away from the hostages.

"Here's how this works. It is three of you and one of me. We are all unarmed. If you three can land a punch or kick on me, you're free to go. If not, well—" Before she could finish the sentence, the three assassins jumped to their feet and attacked.

Ma Sune did not waste time toying with them. After fending off their first attack and causing separation, the first one who came back at her she countered his open palm strike with a death touch. The snoring sound that comes with drowning in one's own blood came instantly. He was dead before he hit the ground.

Seeing their coconspirator fall made the other two change their attack formation. Instead of one taking the frontal and the other the rear assault, both chose to come straight at her. She thrust kicked the first one in the stomach, causing him to double over forward. Then she leaped onto his back and into the air, catching the other one off guard with a spinning roundhouse kick to the chin.

Ma Sune landed on her feet in a crouching position. Tired of fighting, she walked up on the Green Mantis and drew his sword from its sheath. Quickly, she felled both hostages. She wiped the blood off the blade before handing it back to its owner.

"Leave their bodies to fertilize the ground," Ma Sune commanded and walked off. The Green Mantis and Golden Tiger followed in her footsteps. They walked through the compound, moving with a purpose. After checking to see how business was fairing, Ma, accompanied by the two assassins, got in her car and left.

On her way to the destination she had in mind, Ma Sune called Saki. Her niece answered on the first ring. "Master Saki, are you and Master Sia available at the moment?"

"We are in traffic, but we are available," Saki replied.

"Good, meet me at the Lee Clan's compound. It is time we pay Tien Fu Lee a visit," she said.

Saki gave Sia the message. Sia swerved over in the outer lane and got off the expressway. "We are en route. Should we be expecting trouble?" Saki asked.

"Niece, we are trouble. Come prepared for war," Ma Sune replied.

"In the words of an American, already," Saki said and hung up.

Ma pulled over and into a wooded area. She popped the trunk before jumping out of the Benz. She lifted the hood of the trunk, grabbed her sheathed long and short sword and a green silk pouch that was full of ninja stars, and shut the trunk.

"When we get to our destination, show mercy to no one," she said as she sat behind the wheel. She was not looking for a verbal response, and they did not give one either. The Green Mantis and Golden Tiger understood what was expected of them, and they were prepared to perform accordingly.

When she pulled onto the road leading to the Lee Clan's compound, Ma immediately noticed Saki and Sia lounging on the hood of the gloss black with mirror tint windows Lexus Coupe. She pulled over on the side of the road beside the car and got out.

"Masters Saki and Sia Po," Ma Sune said with a bow. "You must not have been too far away. Anyway, shall we proceed on foot from here, seeing the entrance is within walking distance?"

Saki shrugged her shoulders. "I'm just ready to get this over with. What's the plan?"

"No mercy, no revenge. Everything from young to old essence shall wet the blade," Ma replied.

"Five against an entire compound sounds challenging," Sia interjected, understanding what was about to happen. "Anyone care to wager on body count? Just a friendly bet."

"What are you suggesting?" Ma asked.

"I figure, there's at least one hundred eighty bodies inside. Maybe two hundred. Twenty dollars a kill, and the one with the most kills, collect," Sia said.

Saki, Ma, and the two assassins agreed to the terms of the wager.

"Alright, bet on. Let's go have some fun," Saki said. They walked down the road and straight up to the guard's booth near the entrance. After coaxing the guards to open the gates, Sia ended their lives.

"Two for me," Sia said with a smile before walking through the open gates with a ninja star dripping blood in each hand. She spotted two Grey Rhinos in her peripheral. Without thinking twice, Sia threw the two silent death bringers, hitting her targets in the forehead. "Make that four."

Saki, Ma, and the two assassins drew their weapons and spread out in different directions. Each one causing death to linger behind them as they continued to press forward. Sia continued to walk in a straight line. She batted away ninja stars that flew in her direction with the intent to end her life.

Her fearlessness provided a smokescreen for the others to creep inside of the main house and inside of the other buildings. Wherever they entered, it was known because screaming followed by a deadly silence came from within. For it to have only been five of them, they cleared the compound in a short period of time. They met up back out in front of the main house with bloodstains all over their clothes, arms, faces, and swords.

"I want a double or nothing bet back because it is clear you won, Master Sia Po," Ma Sune said. Sia had 89 kills. Everyone else's kills were in the sixties and fifties.

"As you wish, Master Ma Sune. Matter of fact, we are all even. And I'll tell you why," Sia replied. She went on to explain to them how she was killing four to their one or two kills every time. It was her ability to astral project at will that allowed her to do so.

Saki shook her head. "In other words, we never had a winning chance?"

"Not really. Anyway, what are we going to do with this mess? It is a lovely compound," Sia said, looking around at the scenery. There was a nice size garden with rows of iceberg cabbage, mustard greens, snap peas and a variety of peppers growing. On the eastern side of the compound was an acre long vineyard. And the houses were in great condition.

"Well," Ma Sune began saying, "We get the dead bodies and blood cleaned up, it seems like a great start of a new Black Dragon Compound."

That's all Saki needed to hear. She jumped on her phone immediately and called in a cleanup crew. They did not stay around to wait once she provided them with the directions to the Lee Clan's compound.

Willie Slaughter

Chapter Eleven

Jennifer was so upset that she cut herself by accident. *'How could my plans have gone sour?'* she thought. She stopped the bleeding and poured some peroxide on the open wound before she wrapped her left hand in the bandage. Her night had been ruined.

"Juan, did you have something to do with this?" she thought out loud, but then it donned on her. Jennifer ran into her bedroom and over to the walk-in closet. Inside, she opened the secret compartment in the very back of the closet. "So, Tabby, you're back in Jersey? But why?" Jennifer questioned herself. It was already four in the morning, so she stayed up and got ready for work.

She placed the white ninja suit and weapons in the trunk she kept under the bed before going into the kitchen and making her a fruit smoothie. The blend of kiwi and strawberry made for a wild, but pleasant taste. It reminded her of how Tatiana tasted, with the thought, she decided to leave out early to give her a little time with Tatiana.

Jennifer arrived at work at 5:49 a.m. Due to the fact she was early, there were less security checks to go through at the entrance. All she did was flash her federal credentials and state her name, and the security guard opened the gates for her to drive through. But what the guard did do was call, informing the director of Jennifer's arrival like he'd been instructed to.

"I appreciate the call," the director thanked the guard and hung up. He turned his attention to Agent Soledad and Tatiana. "Jennifer's on her way up. Return to your stations. We will finish the meeting later." Both women did as they were asked without speaking a word on their way out of the office.

As soon as Tatiana sat down at her station, the elevator door opened and out came Jennifer, strutting harder than ever. "Hi sexy," she said as she sat on the edge of the desk.

Tatiana made herself smile. "What's good, Jenn? You miss me?"

"How can I not?" she replied seductively. The look in her eyes reflecting her tone. "Anyway, I was thinking about you early this morning, and decided to come in early to spend some time with you."

Tatiana forced a broader smile. "That was very sweet of you, Jenn. So, what's on your mind?"

Jennifer licked her lips. "Maybe we can ride the elevator down to the garage floor at shift change. Huh?"

Tatiana shook her head, laughing. "I do not know, Jenn. You screwed me in the elevator once, and this is the first time I've heard from you since then. We have not even spoken while changing shifts."

Jennifer cringed. "Ouch. You got me there, babe. Let me make it up to you. Please?" She pouted.

Tatiana looked at the time. It was 6:30 a.m. An hour and thirty minutes until shift change. "I do not think anyone's calling this time of the morning. Let's take that elevator ride." She whirled around in the chair and stood to her feet.

"I promise, you will not regret this, babe," Jennifer said while walking beside Tatiana over to the elevator. They stepped inside the elevator. Jennifer pressed the garage floor button, and as soon as the door slid shut, she was all over Tatiana, kissing her lips and unbuttoning her blouse.

"Wait. Slow down, Jenn. It is only six thirty-five," Tatiana said.

"Okay, and I want every second to count," Jennifer replied. She pressed the emergency brake button, causing the elevator to stop. "Strip."

Tatiana did as she was asked. She stood naked inside the elevator. Jennifer shook her head while committing to memory the perfect frame before her. Not being able to resist her craving any longer, she pulled Tatiana down to the floor and mounted her.

Jennifer kissed her passionately while thrusting two of her fingers inside of her. Tatiana moaned as she fingered her. "O, baby. O, Jenn." Tatiana came fast, but Jennifer was not done.

She kissed her way downward, stopping at Tatiana's breasts, which she sucked and bit on each erect nipple teasingly. She kissed her way back up to Tatiana's lips before pressing her sex against hers and hunching.

"Mmm, baby," Jennifer moaned, feeling her release nearing. She hunched harder and faster. Their breasts and bodies melded together like an Oreo, dark and milk chocolate.

Finally, both women trembled violently. They both climaxed, and Jennifer lay on top of her breathing hard. "You bring the best out of me, Tatiana. Why don't you come live with me? We can be together like this every day."

Tatiana smiled and kissed her on the cheek. "No can do, Jenn. I'm not fully committed to the lesbian lifestyle. I like getting some good dick from time to time."

"You're just like all the rest," Jennifer jumped up and said angrily. She dressed quickly.

Tatiana took her time getting dressed. She did not take her eyes off Jennifer. Not that she was scared, but because of her training. "What do you mean I'm just like the rest?"

Jennifer shook her head. "Do not worry about it. I should have never put myself in this predicament again by fucking with another black woman."

"Hold on. Do not go there, Jenn. First and only warning," Tatiana said defensively.

"What?" Jennifer started to say sarcastically. "I said what I said, and I meant it. All y'all black, brown and yellow bitches the same. Do not mind the sex, but ain't trying to make a commitment."

Before Tatiana could stop herself, she had slapped the spit out of Jennifer's mouth. "Consider that a fucking warning. Bitch!"

Jennifer rubbed the right side of her face. She knew from the feel of the slap that she could not beat Tatiana in a fight, so she took her lick and held her tongue.

"What, you tongue-tied now? Go ahead and let your mouth get your ass in some shit it cannot get you out of," Tatiana said angrily. She started the elevator again.

As the door open on their floor and Tatiana was stepping out, Jennifer apologized for the offensive commitment she made, but Tatiana was not trying to hear it. She checked the time. Seeing it was 7:48 a.m., she signed out of the computer, got her things together, and waited for her shift to end.

"Tat, step into my office." Beatrice stuck her head out of the office door and said.

Jennifer could not believe it. She watched Tatiana jumped to her feet and hurried over to the office. *'So, that's the real reason why the bitch will not take me up on my offer,'* she thought. "One more to add to my hit list," she mumbled under her breath.

Inside the office, Beatrice and Tatiana listened to Jennifer mumbling to herself. Due to the high-tech listening device, she planted on Jennifer, they could make out what she was saying.

"Did that mutt just threaten to kill me?" Tatiana asked comically.

Beatrice laughed. "Yeah, but we all know how that'll pan out."

Tatiana looked up at the wall clock. "Well, it is clock out time for me. Hit me up if something interesting touches your eardrums."

"Gotcha sis. Stay on point," Beatrice replied.

Tatiana walked out the office. Before the office door closed behind her, she spun around and caught it, and swiftly stepped back inside. Agent Soledad beckoned for her to come over to where she sat listening in on the conversation.

"You must've heard my thoughts," Beatrice said.

"Something like that. When I peeped who she was kicking it with, I figured it would be interesting to hear," Tatiana replied. They sat quietly, listening to Jennifer and Juan's conversation. Afterward, Agent Soledad picked up the phone receiver and called the director's extension.

"Director Wade Stevens. How may I help you?" he answered the line and said.

"Wade, it is Beatrice. I'm on my way over to your office," she replied and hung up. "Alright Young Master Tarnish, I'll see you later. Do not forget we have a meeting to finish."

Tatiana nodded. "10-4, Master Chalice." She hurried out the door, passing by Jennifer, who was getting all mushy with Juan, she sucked her teeth and rolled her eyes to add humor to an emotion she really did not feel at the moment. She had no feelings for Jennifer. If it was left up to her, Jennifer would be dead already.

Tatiana put extra sway to her hips as she stomped, making the sound of the six-inch heels echo as she walked towards the elevator. When she entered the elevator and turned to face the closing door, she noticed both Jennifer and Juan staring at her. Both eyes filled with lust.

'I could kill both of you right now,' she thought.

Jennifer tapped on Juan's leg to get his attention. She realized he was lusting after Tatiana as she was. "So, you're fucking Tat, too? After all the love shit you talk to me about while and after fucking me?" Although her tone was low and calm, her eyes showed the true fury.

"No, I have not slept with Tatiana. She wouldn't give me a chance to even speak on that level. Besides, I'm real with it. You're the only woman I'm screwing," Juan said.

Jennifer smiled. "You're the only loyal person on my team. So, do you have any info for me?"

Juan shook his head. "Everything is on the hush around the office. However, I was able to get the other mission completed. I gave the crew your address, so expect them to drop by around midnight." Juan heard an office door open and looked up to see Agent Soledad walking out of her office, heading for the director's office. "Good morning, Agent Soledad." She responded by the nod of her head without breaking stride. After the door closed behind her, Agent Santiago frowned and said, "She is a real strange one."

"I know, right?" Jennifer replied, thinking that maybe Agent Soledad and Tatiana were lovers. *'More of a reason to kill her, too,'* she thought she was thinking to herself until Juan stood.

"What do you mean kill her, too? What do you got going on, Jenn?" he asked.

"Anyway," Jennifer said, not giving any thought to his questions. "You said they'll be over at midnight tonight?"

He nodded hesitantly. "Yeah, tonight. Are you going to tell me what's really going down? If we are in this together, then I need to be prepared for whatever might come my way."

Jennifer thought long and hard on just how much she wanted to reveal to him. She stared Juan directly in the eyes. "Okay, I'll fill you in. But, the first sign I see of you getting cold feet on me, your pussy supply will be cut off. Do you understand me?"

"Yeah, I understand. So, what's up?" Juan said as he sat back down on the edge of the desk. "I'm all ears."

Jennifer gave him a quick rundown on her vendetta and plans for vengeance against her ex-lover and her ex-lover's family and friends. "One side of the nigger's family is already deceased. The only one left is Tabitha Greene."

"So, what does this Malice character have to do with any of this? And why drag an assassin's guild and Asians into your personal beef?" Juan asked, not fully understanding Jennifer's disdain for everyone other than Tabitha Greene. He really was not feeling the racial remarks either, but he let it slide, hoping she wouldn't use the word again.

Jennifer took a deep breath and exhaled. "Because they took my Tabby away from me. She loved me and I loved her before she met the bastards. So, I am going to take everything away from her, and when she comes crawling back to me, I'm going to thrust a blade through her heart."

Juan swallowed. The woman he thought he knew did not exist in his mind anymore. He was starting to see Jennifer for the psychopath she was, but it was too late. He'd already fallen for her, and he knew she knew it.

"So, are you still in love with me, Agent Santiago?" Jennifer asked.

"Why shouldn't I be? Listen, I gotta get to work. We will catch up at lunch if you're up to it," Juan said as he stood up to leave.

Jennifer nodded with a smile, showing two rows of perfect white teeth. "You know I'm down with you, boo. I'll see you at lunch."

Juan smiled and walked off.

Director Wade Stevens and Agent Soledad had overheard the entire conversation between Jennifer and Agent Santiago. They sat in silence, thinking about the course of action they wanted to take. While in deep thought, Wade's personal cellphone began vibrating on top of his desk.

"Hello?" he picked up and answered.

"Master Diablo, this is Ken. Any news of the nuisance?" the caller said.

"Matter of fact, it is. I and Master Chalice just finish overhearing a conversation between her and her accomplice," Diablo replied.

"Interesting. What's good?" Ken said.

"A team of hitters are going to be at the residence around midnight tonight. We already know who her ally is within the agency. How would you like for us to proceed in dealing with the ally?" Diablo responded.

"Terminate it. We will deal with the rest," Ken replied and hung up.

Diablo hung up the phone and nodded to Chalice. "He's all yours."

Chalice smiled and left out of the office. On her way back to her office, she spoke to Jennifer, who waved back before answering the phone. Inside the office, she unplugged the phone and relaxed in her maroon high back leather chair. *'This will be easy,'* she thought as she closed her eyes.

Chalice deepened her meditative state. It took her three minutes to reach the level of concentration needed to start and finish the mission at hand. She astral projected and stood looking at her physical body for a brief moment before walking through the wall leading to Agent Santiago's office. Coming to stand inside his office, she wielded her favorite weapon, the chain-link sickle.

Juan was sitting behind his desk talking to a client over the phone. He had no idea how close death was until Chalice expertly wielded her weapon, snatching his life away from him. The phone receiver fell from his hand before his face hit the desk, he was dead.

Chalice opened her eyes with a smile on her face. She took a few deep breaths before standing. A little wobbly on her feet, she walked out of her office.

"Agent Soledad, do you have a moment?" Jennifer asked, seeing her headed for the director's office.

"Not at the moment," she replied without breaking stride.

"And why not?" Jennifer asked with more aggression in her tone than wanted.

"You should pay more attention to time before it slips away from you, Jenn. It is lunch break," Agent Soledad said as she opened the door to the director's office and walked inside.

Jennifer, disturbed by Beatrice's nonchalant attitude, looked at the time in the bottom right-hand corner of the desktop computer. It was lunchtime, which was confusing because she was waiting for Agent Santiago who normally would have walked out of his office ten minutes ago. Before she realized her own actions, she was standing at Juan's office door, knocking.

"Agent Santiago, it is time for lunch break," Jennifer said as she opened the door and stuck her head inside. Seeing the phone receiver dangling and Juan's head face down on the desk, she walked in with caution. "Agent Santiago?" Jennifer touched his hand, and immediately knew he was dead. "Oh, my god! Somebody call an ambulance!" She ran out of the office screaming. She barged in the director's office screaming the same thing.

Wade and Beatrice were eating salads and talking about the upcoming presidential election. They took one good look at her and frowned. "Slow down, Jenn. What's the problem?" Director Stevens said without a hint of true concern in his voice.

"Did you not hear what I fucking said? Agent Santiago is dead!" Jennifer was hysterical.

"Agent Soledad, go check it out," Wade said. Beatrice closed the lid on her salad and did as she was asked. She came back a minute later. "Yup, he's definitely not ticking. I've called the coroner to come get the body. I also called in a team to comb through his office to make sure the cause of death was not an illegal substance he chose to use."

"Great job and thank you, Agent Soledad," Director Stevens said before turning his attention to Jennifer. "Situation taken care of, Jenn. Go enjoy your lunch."

Jennifer was fuming with hate inside. "Can y'all not see what's happening here? Agent Santiago is dead! A healthy man is fucking dead, and I'm more than sure it was them goddam assassins!"

"Calm your nerves or get out of my office. Nobody got time to be listening to fairy tales about ninjas in New Jersey," Wade warned.

"Yes, sir. I apologize, sir. I am out of line. Enjoy your salad, sir," Jennifer said sarcastically before storming out of the office.

Wade looked at Beatrice who hunched her shoulders while forking a cherry. "Piece of cake. I could've taken her out, too."

"I know, but that's not how he wants it done," Wade replied.

They returned to eating their salads and talking politics. All the while, their thoughts were on putting an end to the nuisance of a secretary slash agent sitting in the corridor.

Willie Slaughter

Chapter Twelve

Kenneth hung up the phone and returned to watching Yuri show Miranda how to wield the bow staff properly. To everyone's astonishment, she was a quick learner. Their training session was very entertaining, but Kenneth's mind was somewhere else.

He turned to his wife, and asked, "Have anyone seen Tabitha this morning?"

Angela shook her head. "I have not. How about you, Yishi? You seen, Tabitha?"

Yishi responded by shaking her head. She was in deep thought about the training session.

"Before you ask, no, I have not seen Tabitha Green," Qi said after overhearing the question asked twice.

Kenneth's grandmother overhead them questioning the whereabouts of Tabitha. She had personally made sure the other guests were fed. But what she had not done was wake her granddaughter. Before her presence was known, she stepped back inside from the courtyard and went straight to Tabitha's room.

"Tabitha, wake up baby," she said while tapping Tabitha on the shoulder.

Her eyelids fluttered open. She sat straight up in bed, yawning and stretching. "I'm awake. What time is it?"

"Time for you to get yourself together. You have guests to tend to, and Kenny and the others are in the courtyard. They are trying to figure out where you are," her grandmother replied.

Tabitha got on up and went into the bathroom. She brushed her teeth, washed her face and used the toilet. Although she had slept for a good 10 hours, her body still craved more rest.

'The price you pay for knowing how to do certain shit,' she thought.

"Are you okay, baby?" her grandmother asked. Looking in Tabitha's eyes, she could see the weariness.

"I'm good, Nana. It is the blunt of working late at night. It gets the butter from the duck sometimes," Tabitha replied.

"Yeah, I bet it does," she said with concern. "Are you hungry? I had the cook make blueberry waffles, bacon strips, eggs, orange juice, and coffee. Oh, and tea of course."

Tabitha smiled. "Thanks, I'll have all the above. However, after I go talk to Tabitha and Trent."

"Do not worry child, I'll have it brought out to you. Let me show you another route to the rooms across from the courtyard, so you will not be seen," her grandmother said.

The two left out the room taking in casual conversation while they walked down the hallway. Not really paying attention to where they were going, Tabitha had missed everything. All she knew was she found herself standing in the room with her grandmother and the couple who sat watching television.

"I'll go get your breakfast, Tabitha," her grandmother said and left the same way they'd come.

"I hope you're enjoying your stay," Tabitha said to her guests.

"It is better than any motel or hotel I've ever stayed at," Trent replied.

Tabitha took his comment as a compliment. "After I eat my breakfast, I'm going to take you to meet the rest of the fam."

Tabitha pointed out the window. "You mean the people out there training?"

"Who and what are they, some kind of martial art masters? Ninjas?" Trent asked.

"Something like that. Why you ask?" Tabitha said.

Trent's expression turned serious. "Because my fiancé and I have degrees in Ancient Mui Thai. That what they are doing is more like Ninja."

Tabitha nodded with a look of impressed on her face. "That means you two will fit right in."

"Here's your breakfast young lady," her grandmother chimed in coming through a different passage than before. She sat the tray filled with waffles, bacon strips and eggs and orange juice on the table and left.

Tabitha sat down at the table and dug in. She did not say a word or lift her head until the tray was empty of food and drink. She belched. "Excuse me." She stood and stretched for a moment. "Alright, let's go meet the rest of the team."

They walked out the front door that put them in view of everyone in the courtyard. Angela spotted her first and nudged Kenneth in the side. "There goes little miss busy body and looks like she is made new friends."

"Definitely not what we need, right now," Kenneth said before getting up and walking over to meet his cousin and the couple with her. His wife, Yishi, Trent and Qi brought up his rear. "Tab, who you got here?"

Tabitha bowed. "I apologize for being late, but I went on a scouting mission last night. Masters Sun, Shyan, Yishi, Trent, and Qi, meet Tabitha and Trent. Tabitha and Trent, meet Masters' Sun, Shyan, Yishi, Trent, and Qi."

They bowed to each other. Yishi was the first to catch on to their names. "Did you say, Tabitha and Trent? What a coincidence."

"Not really. Jennifer was out to kill them because of their names. I just so happened to be in the right place at the right time," Tabitha replied. She looked over at Miranda and Yuri who was training her with the bow staff. "How is she coming along?"

"Great. She is a fast learner," Yishi said. "What about these two? What are they prepared to do?"

"Why don't we let Master Trent and you find out, Master Yishi Pe Sune?" Tabitha replied. She called Miranda and Yuri over to meet Trent and Tabitha. Yuri automatically started looking from the couple to the Tabitha and Trent he knew. "Somebody got to gain some nicknames because I'm not about to attempt to know who is looking for who in the near future. Anyway, nice meeting you kindred spirits."

Yishi said something to Yuri in Mandarin that caused him to bow and remain silent. She turned her attention to Trent and Tabitha. "Will we be doing martial combat or weaponry?"

"Martial," Tabitha interjected and answered for the couple.

Yishi nodded. "Okay then, let's go. Master Trent, shall we?"

Trent did not say a word. He walked out to stand in the middle of the courtyard. Yishi hurried over and stood beside him. The couple stepped out in front of them. Tabitha facing off with Yishi and her fiancé stood before Trent.

Kenneth was about to go over Tu rules when his grandmother and grandfather came out carrying Long Island Teas, sipping on them through straws. "Ooh, I think I know how this match goes." his grandfather said while sitting in the lounge chair. "Watch out, Kenny, let me do it."

Everybody's attention went to his and Tabitha's grandparents. "What?" the old man said. "Y'all ain't the only people who know how to get down with the get down. Take notes."

"Let's see what you got, Pops," Kenneth said and moved to the side. His grandfather grunted as if to clear his throat. "It seems as if we have a martial duel. The rules are this. Whichever opponent taps first, the principle of that opponent must stand aside and allow their counterpart to continue the duel against their principle. If there be a draw, meaning, if a principle wins on each team, the martial combat evolves into a match of weaponry proficiency.

"Do we have an understanding of the rules, ladies, and gentlemen?" Both teams faced him and bowed. "Great, let the match begin," the old man said. Everyone, except Tabitha, was astounded. "What are you staring at us for? The entertainment is in the middle of the courtyard."

Kenneth smirked. "Yeah, Pops, me, you Grandma and Tab will have this conversation later."

"Oh, be quiet boy. We are trying to enjoy the afternoon," his grandmother said. "This is going to be good. Any bets?"

Kenneth felt his wife's comforting strong grip about his right shoulder. She did not have to say anything for him to understand what it meant. He turned around and watched the match getting ready to unfold. The teams bowed to one another.

The match began. Tabitha and Trent started off showing their skills, being long term partners. They gripped each other's forearms and began hurling each other in the direction of their opponents. Yishi and Trent had to separate in order to evade the attack.

"Shadow Dragon," Yishi said in Chinese.

Trent nodded his head, showing he understood. Before the couple could truly understand what was going on, Yishi came leaping high through the air from their right and Trent from the left. They readied themselves for an aerial attack, but it was the illusion Yishi and Trent hoped they went for. They joined hands in passing through the air and landed with their arms locked around their opponents.

"What in the hell kind of attack was that?" the old man said almost dropping his drink.

"That's that I'll kick your ass technique," Tabitha said with enthusiasm.

The couple tried to wiggle their way out of the captivity Yishi and Trent had them in, but could not. They gave up and yielded to defeat. Yishi and Trent unlocked their hold and bowed towards their opponents and then towards the spectators.

"What art was that? I've never seen anything like it," Tabitha admitted.

"Shadow Dragon, it is a technique developed by us through our kindred spirits. You fight well in the way you have been trained, however, if you're truly to be of our family, you must learn the way of and embrace the Black Dragon and Green Mantis Spirit within you," Yishi said.

"We accept the offer and we are willing to learn," Tabitha replied.

Yishi nodded. "Very well then. Since we are all here, I do believe Master Kenneth has some prominent information for us. Master Kenneth?"

Kenneth stood before them and bowed. "Yes, I do. Masters Diablo, Chalice and Tarnish of the Guild gave me the 4-1-1 on Jennifer's plans and allies. One of whom was an Agent Juan Santiago. He's no longer with us, by the way, thanks to Master Chalice—"

"Yes, that's my little sister," Angela cut her husband off saying. She could feel his eyes staring at her. "I apologize, bae. What were you saying?"

He grinned and continued, "Like I was saying before I was rudely interrupted by my wonderful queen, the agent named, Juan Santiago is no longer with us. Master Diablo has informed me of a meeting that's supposed to go down around midnight tonight at Jennifer's crib. She is putting together her own little team of hitters.

"I guess my question to the family is. How would you like to deal with it?"

His grandmother raised her hand. "Do I have a say so in the matter, Kenny?"

Kenneth sighed. The more he thought about it, he knew it was a bad idea allowing his and Tabitha's grandparents to attend such a meeting. "Of course, you do Grandma. What's up?"

She took a sip of the Long Island Tea and handed her husband the glass before standing. "From what I gather out of this, there are three new members to the fam. They need to get the feel of some true action. It is the only way to know if they are family criteria."

"Tell it, Nana," Tabitha butted in.

"Tabitha Greene be quiet while I'm talking," the old woman demanded and continued to speak, "I ain't saying they ain't built for this family. I'm saying they need the field experience, so they'll know what's expected of them when it comes down to the get down."

Kenneth was speechless for a moment. To hear his grandparents speak on a lifestyle, he never could imagine them knowing about or living was baffling. "So, what do you propose?"

"Take them with y'all tonight. Show them what Shadow Dragon will really do to the enemy," she replied.

"And what do you have to say, Pops?" Kenneth asked his grandfather.

"Kenny, if you do not take any advice from me, take what I'm about to tell you as a golden rule. Matter of fact, all men present take heed to what an old man is going to say. You gotta know when and when not to. If your woman don't ask for your advice, keep your mouth closed," he said and sipped his tea.

"Well, that's settled. Miranda, Tabitha, and Trent welcome to the family. And since we are learning new things about each other, Ma and Pops, my name is Sun Sune, and Tabitha's name is Moon Tao Po. Which is great knowing since there's another Tabitha now," Kenneth said.

"Well, I'll be damned. Sun and Moon. Y'all could not have gotten better names," his grandfather replied.

It was only 2:11 p.m. They all decided to shower and meet in the dining room for an afternoon meal.

Chapter Thirteen

Ma Sune had called and spoken to Zhia about what had taken place. Zhia was upset. Not because of the attempt made by the Lee Clan and the renegade Wen Clan members. She was mad because she was not part of the party to slaughter them.

"We should go have a personal sit down with Master Lin Su Wen," Zhia said. Her tone was not being optional but demanding the meeting.

"When?" Ma Sune asked.

"Now," she answered and hung up.

Ma Sune sat the phone on the desk. *'This is usually my meditation hour,'* she thought as she left her study. On her way to her sleeping quarters to retrieve her weapons, she saw Saki and Sia training under the moonlight. She stood still watching them from a distance, admiring their dedication to the art.

"Masters Saki and Sia Po," she said to get their attention. "Do you care to accompany me and Master Zhia Mi Yang to Master Lin Su Wen's compound?"

The two masters ceased with their training and walked over to where Ma Sune stood. Both agreed to go with her and Zhia.

"As always, it is an honor having you two around. Master Zhia Mi Yang should be here shortly. We will take one of the Hummers. Until she gets here, relax. I'm more than sure you'll have plenty of Wen Clan members to practice your skills on," Ma said before heading for her sleeping quarters.

When she returned to the place she'd left Saki and Sia, Zhia was standing with them dressed in a solid gold ninja suit holding the mask in her left hand. Saki and Sia were dressed in their solid black ninja suits without masks on. Ma, in the forest green ninja suit, smiled inside.

"Before we leave, it will be a great honor to have a picture taken of us for a wonderful memory," Ma Sune said and called for one of the Green Mantises to take their picture with her iPhone 11. The assassin waited until she was standing between Saki and Zhia with Sia on the other side of Saki before he started snapping away.

The Green Mantis snapped ten pictures from different angles before handing her back the phone and disappearing in the shadows.

"I'll have the pictures blown up and printed out first thing in the morning. Let's go, ladies," Ma Sune said and started walking towards the front gate. Zhia, Saki and Sia were at her sides.

Waiting outside the gates near a Hummer was a Green Mantis. The assassin opened the rear driver's side door for them and closed it once they were comfortably in. Ma Sune told the assassin their destination. He jumped behind the wheel of the SUV and drove them there.

Instead of announcing their presence upon arrival, the four deadly masters put on their masks, grabbed their gear, and hopped out of the vehicle a quarter of a mile up the road. They used grappling hooks to scale the wall in order to gain entrance undetected and unknowingly. Once in, the four assassins took out blow dart guns and used them to eliminate the first hostiles they came in contact with. The poison tip darts buried themselves inside the necks of the targets, causing instant death.

Using the grace and silence of a cat, Ma Sune, Saki, Zhia, and Sia continued forward. When the next targets were in sight, they pulled out two ninja stars a piece and threw the silent instruments of death. The stars cut through the crisp and cool night air and met their destinations with an unkindly greeting.

The Wen assassins fell from the balcony, dead before hitting the ground.

Before taking another step, the four masters unsheathed their blades. The glint of the steel in the moonlight looked mystical. As they pressed forward, the illuminance of the steel became dull from the blood of all within their path. They found themselves inside Master Lin Su Wen's house in no time.

In pairs, they left a trail of dead bodies and blood leading up both sides of the double stairwell. Maids, assassins, animals, all fell under the thrust or slashing of their blades. They approached the master bedroom door with caution. Intimate sounds could be heard inside, which made for a great cover in their minds.

Saki and Sia were posted on the left side of the door. Ma Sune and Zhia on the right. Saki nodded, giving her aunt the go-ahead. Ma grabbed the doorknob and turned it slowly and gently pushed the door open to a crack.

She looked through the crack, and sure enough, Lin Su Wen had a young lover with her. She was bucking on top of him hard and fast. The four assassins entered the room and closed the door behind them without making a sound. Ma Sune, Saki, and Sia lay flat on their stomachs and crawled over to the side of the bed while Zhia crept up behind Lin Su Wen from the foot of the bed.

As Zhia wrapped the razor spiked coil around Lin Su Wen's neck, strangling her, Ma, Sia, and Saki emerged and ran their blades through Lin's lover. Her eyes began to bulge from the lack of oxygen. The more she tried to resist, the razors on the coil sliced through her throat. Zhia could've made her death less painful, but she did not for her own selfish reasons.

Finally, Lin Su Wen could not resist death any longer. Her strength failed her, and her arms dropped to her sides as her eyes locked in the stare of death. It happened right as an orgasm was claiming her body from the stimulating length of her lover's manhood. Having their mission complete, the two Black Dragons, the Green Mantis, and Golden Tiger left the Wen Clan's compound.

"Assemble a platoon, and go clean up the mess," Ma Sune commanded before getting out. The Green Mantis nodded and drove off.

"Well, there's another free compound. What are we going to do with so much property?" Sia said.

"We expand. Saki, you and Yishi shall take as many warriors and help you need to govern Lin Su Wen's compound and business. I do believe they were into the export and import distillery business. Sia, you and Moon can do the same thing with the Lee Clan's compound," Ma Sune replied.

"Looks like we are monopolizing," Zhia began saying. "Which is a great start of a new High Council. Those who refuse to abide by the rules shall taste death. Soon, this might turn out to be a Black Dragon, Green Mantis and Golden Tiger ran country."

"Sounds great to me," Saki said.

"Me too," Ma agreed. She looked up at the moon. "Master Zhia Mi Yang, it is late. Why don't you stay here and be my company for the remainder of this moon?"

"You know I will, Master Ma Sune," she replied. They walked off, leaving Saki and Sia standing under the moonlit sky.

"We are about to have our own compounds," Saki said voice filled with excitement. She hugged her cousin.

"That we are, cousin. Just try to remain mindful of how we obtained them, so we do not lose them," Sia replied.

Saki understood exactly what she meant. It was through bloodshed they gained the compounds and only by shedding more blood would they keep it.

***

Jennifer was sulking through the rest of her day. The one guy she was screwing was dead and Tatiana had given her the boot. *'What a shitty day,'* she thought when the phone rang. "Hello? Jennifer speaking."

"Hi Jenn," the caller said. Her voice caused Jennifer's heart to skip a beat. She was speechless. "Jenn, are you there? Is everything alright?"

When her speech did return, it was almost a whisper. "Tabby, why? Why did you do this to me? I loved you."

"Listen, I was just calling to check up on you. I see you're back at work and in great physical health. Have a—"

"No, wait," Jennifer cut her off. "Can we meet someplace after I get off of work?"

Tabitha laughed. "I highly doubt it, Jenn."

"Why not?" Jennifer asked. "Are you seeing someone?"

"Of course, I am. Sia and I are in a healthy relationship. We are getting married soon," Tabitha lied. The healthy relationship part was the truth, but not the marriage portion. She could tell by the sound of Jennifer's breathing that she was on the verge of losing it mentally and emotionally, which was part of her plan.

"I knew you and that bitch was having an affair," Jennifer said angrily. "But that's okay. By the time I'm finished with y'all black bitches, you're going to wish you never crossed me."

Tabitha laughed harder. "Stop it, Jenn. You're killing me."

"Oh, but I'm planning on doing just that, you, black bitch," Jennifer replied.

"If you say so. Don't forget you're in a federal building, therefore, all calls are subject to being monitored and recorded," Tabitha stated and hung up.

Hearing the line go dead, Jennifer slammed the cordless phone down on the desk repeatedly until it cracked.

The director just so happened to be coming out of his office and witnessed the whole breakdown. "Jennifer, are you okay? You've been edgy around here lately."

"My girlfriend left me for a mixed breed, the man I was fucking is dead, and my new girlfriend just slapped and left me today. Hell no, I'm not okay," she answered drooling out the mouth.

In Wade Stevens's mind, it was a sure sign of mental health issues. "Sorry, Jennifer, but I'm going to have to send you home for the rest of the day. You're emotionally and mentally stressed, and I'm afraid it'll interfere with you doing your job properly. Come back tomorrow morning, and if you do not appear to be in better spirits, I'm putting you in for a psych evaluation."

"But—" Jennifer started to say, but he cut her off.

"There's no buts in this conversation. Get your things together and leave the premises," he warned.

"Sir, yes sir," she said in a tone of defeat. She never brought anything of importance to work, so she just got up and left. *'It is better that I go prepare for tonight anyway,'* she thought as she walked through the parking garage. Her heels were clanking loudly against the concrete, but she stopped and stood still because of a shadow moving in her peripheral vision.

"Whoever is there, you can come out. You're not scaring me," Jennifer said. There was no response, so she continued forward to her 911 Porsche. As soon as she grabbed the door handle, a ninja star buried itself inside the exterior of the driver's side door. Jennifer jumped out of fear. As her hands trembled, she opened the door, slid behind the wheel, and slammed the door shut.

Jennifer started the engine and gunned for the exit. Hearing the tires of the vehicle screeching, Tarnish stepped out of the shadows with a smile on her face.

Willie Slaughter

Chapter Fourteen

It was 6:19 p.m. night was approaching fast. Everyone sat at the dinner table at Freeman's Estate. Sun and Moon's grandfather was being an entertainer.

"For those of you who do not know, my name is Paul Fitzgerald Freeman, and this lovely lady here is my wife Margaret Geneva Freeman. But, since you're all brothers and sisters of our knucklehead grands, it is cool to call us Pops and Nana," he said after performing a gentleman's bow.

Paul told them a story about him being active in The Cold War. Everybody gave him their undivided attention. "Yeah. it was the worst damn war I fought in next to winning your granny's heart."

That got a good-natured laugh from everybody except Yishi, Yuri and Shyan.

"Seriously, I regret ever having fought in The Cold War. A lot of us good old colored people regret it," Paul stated and sighed.

"If you do not mind me asking," Yishi began. "What makes it so regrettable?"

"That's the million-dollar question, Yishi. When you learn you're fighting to keep your own kind enslaved, there's no greater shame," he replied. The memory took him there emotionally. "Men, y'all care to join me in the den? I need a drink." Paul stood up and started towards the door.

Both Trents, Sun, Yuri, and Qi followed behind him, leaving the women at the dining table.

"I hope they do not get too drunk," Tabitha said.

Margaret bust out laughing. "Child, there's no such thing as a Freeman getting too drunk. They handle their liquor, and they definitely know how to take care of their women."

Shyan, being in agreement, waved her hand over her head. "Amen to that. Besides, they know what's up. Business is pleasure at the end of the day."

***

Ma Sune and Zhia were breathless from pleasing each other. They lay cuddling. Ma's thoughts were on her daughter Yishi, her nephews Qi and Yuri. Zhia knew by the intensity of the lovemaking.

"What's on your mind, lover?" Zhia asked.

"Ready for my daughter and nephews to return home. They've been in the United States longer than I expected them to be," she replied.

"Why don't you call to see what's taking so long?" Zhia asked.

"I think I'll take your advice," Ma Sune said. She rolled over and grabbed her phone from the night lampstand. Scrolling through her contacts, she found Yishi's name and called.

"Hello?" Yishi answered on the first ring.

"Master Yishi Pe Sune, this is your mother. What seems to be the hold up on your return home?" she said in Mandarin.

"Mother, we are working towards completing the task this moon," Yishi replied with confidence.

"Here's some wisdom, my daughter. If you take one's kingdom away, you've taken their strength. Eventually, they will self-destruct on their own. Do what's necessary and come home," Ma Sune said demandingly.

"I'll present your wise words to the rest. I'm more than certain they'll also see the wisdom as I do," her daughter replied.

"See you soon, Yishi," she said before hanging up. Ma Sune sat the phone back on the stand.

"What's the verdict?" Zhia asked.

Ma rolled over and began kissing and squeezing on Zhia's breasts. "They are just fine. Now, let me make you feel happier." She massaged Zhia's body with her lips and hands with a passion Zhia was not accustomed to. All she could do was moan and tremble from the orgasms claiming her body from the gentle touch of Ma Sune's lips against her clitoris.

"Ma. Ma. I love you," she spoke in between moans. Her declaration of love motivated Ma Sune to love all over her body longer. After giving Zhia an extensive amount of pleasure, she resigned to rubbing her clitoris against Zhia's until she came.

"I love you so much, Ma Sune," Zhia stated while holding her in her embrace.

"And I love you, too, Zhia Mi Yang. Let's get some rest. In the morning, we have much work to do," Ma replied.

"You're moving them out so soon?" Zhia asked teasingly.

"They deserve their space and so do we," she said.

They cuddled until they fell asleep.

***

Jennifer stopped at the sport's bar to have a drink on her way home. While sipping on the strong gin on ice, she thought about calling to try and patch things up with Tatiana Remembering the slap in the face made her change her mind. She was sitting at the bar, drinking and watching the seconds tick away on the clock when a female walked over and sat down beside her.

"A strawberry wine cooler, please," the lady ordered. "And get my friend here whatever she is drinking." The tall brunette swirled around on the barstool to face Jennifer. "My name is Billie."

Jennifer eyed her from head to toe. Billie was a well-built 5'11 and 175 pounds with pale blue eyes. A real looker. *'Maybe I got myself a real girlfriend here,'* she thought. "I'm Jennifer."

"Nice meeting you Jennifer. I could not help but notice you sitting alone. Are you friendly?" Billie said in a way that Jennifer would understand what she was really asking.

"That depends," Jennifer replied. Before either knew it, they were at Jennifer's spot stripping each other out of the clothes surrounding the package they were so ready to taste and touch.

"Billie, are you going to play with my emotions? If so, tell me straight up this is a one-night-stand," Jennifer said in a serious tone of voice.

"I'm single and I take it you're single, too. Let's make the best of it," Billie replied and playfully pushed Jennifer on the bed.

They tongued each other down passionately while rubbing body to body. Jennifer sighed from the pleasant feel of Billie's breast and sex pressed against hers. Her long hair acted as a shield about their faces, shrouding their moans and stares into one another's eyes. It was a moment of bliss.

They took their lovemaking from the bed to the Jacuzzi, and back to the bed, where they climaxed together one last time before laying silently within each other's arms.

"Jennifer, would you like for me to stay the night?" she asked.

"Oh, shit!" Jennifer exclaimed, remembering what was happening at midnight. She looked at the clock. It was 11:28 p.m. "Billie, I would love for you too, but not tonight."

Billie propped herself up on her right elbow. "There's someone else isn't there? I knew this was too damn good to be true."

"No, no. There's no one else," Jennifer said while touching her on the cheek. "I have some business to tend to in a little while. My contacts are expecting me to be home alone."

Billie embraced her hand against her cheek. "Tell me anything, baby."

"After tonight is over, you can move in with me," Jennifer promised. She looked at the clock again. It was fifteen minutes until midnight. "Matter of fact, pack your shit tonight, and bring it on over around ten in the morning."

Billie got up and got dressed. She kissed Jennifer passionately on the lips before showing herself out. Jennifer lay in bed happier than ever. What a night, she thought.

Billie inserted the key into the lock and was about to unlock the car door when she heard the sound of a twig snap behind her. "Jennifer, is that you?" No response came. As she turned back around to face the door, she jumped back out of fright.

"What in the hell are you?" Billie said through quivering lips.

The figure crouched on the roof of the car and did not respond. All Billie could see was the whites of the eyes. The rest of the body was covered in black. She tried to turn and flee but found herself staring in the eyes of another unknown masked figure.

Before Billie could muster up the strength to scream, the assassin thrust the blade of the dagger through her jugular vein. The blood began squirting out the side of her neck as she fell to the ground. Her killer said something in Chinese, and two more assassins appeared out of the shadows and took the lifeless corpse away. Once the body was removed, the assassins disappeared under the cloak of the dark skies.

They waited in the shadows for their targets to arrive. They did not arrive a moment too late. Two dark blue Dodge Caravans pulled up in front of Jennifer's house. Once the lights and engines were turned off, the ten assassins started creeping through the shadows.

The driver, passenger and sliding rear door of the Caravans opened, and out stepped ten men carrying concealed firearms. Seeing the weapons, the assassins took precautions and spread out. Each one took out two ninja stars, readying them, waiting on the perfect moment. The moment came as the doors of the vehicles were being closed.

The ten assassins released the instruments of death in the air. Neither fell short of finding a place within the flesh. Having gained the upper hand, they quickly emerged from the shadows and finished what they'd started. Although the gunmen were already dying, they wet their blades in their blood.

The smallest of the assassins waited on the others to do as they planned with the bodies before running up to the front door and ringing the doorbell several times and flipping back into the shadows. The door came open and Jennifer stepped out onto the front porch. She saw the vans and the silhouettes of their passengers. A broad smile was on her face as she walked over to meet her team.

"Get out and come inside," Jennifer said in a commanding way as she approached the passenger side of the first van. The man did not move, and his lack of obeying her got the best of her temper. "I said—" She stopped mid-sentence after snatching the door open and the body falling out to the ground.

Panic immediately caused adrenaline to flood her bloodstream. Jennifer, out of curiosity, opened the rear sliding door. Seeing the lifeless corpses piled inside, she freaked out and had a panic attack. While she was whizzing, trying to catch her breath, two of the assassins carried Billie's body inside of the house, laid it across the bed, and crept back outside undetected.

Jennifer calmed herself as much as the situation allowed her to and ran back inside. She hurried to the bedroom to get her cellphone. But when she bent the corner and stepped in the room, she screamed. There, lying across the bed, was Billie's dead body with eyes staring in her direction.

"Billie! No!" she screamed and dropped to her knees in the doorway. "No!" Jennifer continued to cry.

She wiped her eyes with the back of her right hand, smearing mascara all over her face. Right as she muscled up the strength to stand again, the *Dangerously In Love* ringtone began playing on her phone. Filled with fury mixed with fear, Jennifer walked on wobbly legs to where the phone lay on top of the dresser.

"Hello?" her voice quivered through the phone.

"Jenn, why do you sound so, I do not know, scared and lonely?" the caller asked humorously.

The sound of Tabitha's voice turned her fear to rage. "You nigger, bitch! Why don't you come fight me head up? You've taken everything from me. Come kill me and get it over with!"

"That would be a waste of energy, Jenn. Besides, in my mind, you're already dead. You're a devil without pawns," Tabitha replied.

"So, you think bitch! As long as I'm living, you and your family are on my hit list bitch," Jennifer warned.

"Yeah, whatever. Goodbye." Tabitha hung up.

Willie Slaughter

Chapter Fifteen

The following morning, Jennifer woke up to a hell storm. The sound of doors being broken down and windows being shattered. Before she could wrap her mind around what was happening, three heavily armed FBI agents stormed in the bedroom with weapons aimed her way.

"Freeze! Do not move!" one of the agents yelled. One of the other agents radioed in they had suspect contained. A male's voice came back over the receiver letting them know he was on the way in. Jennifer knew the voice of Director Wade Stevens from anywhere.

"What in the hell is this?" he walked in and said, seeing Jennifer laying in the bed next to the dead body. "Jennifer, would you like to explain how there's two vans filled with dead bodies in your driveway?"

Jennifer looked a mess. Mascara was all over her face, clothes bloody and hair wild and matted with dry blood. "I was just about to get ready for work, sir."

The director frowned. "Ma'am, you have some serious problems at the moment, and neither states you should be considering work. Cuff her and bring her in."

Two of the agents held her at gunpoint while the other placed the restraints on her. It did not don on her what was happening until she felt the cold steel lock around her wrists.

"What are you doing? Get your damn hands off me! I'm a federal employee!" Jennifer tried to resist.

"Correction, you were a federal employee. Take her away," Director Stevens said.

Two of the FBI agents concealed their firearms before hefting Jennifer's body in the air and onto their shoulders. She squirmed violently, trying to wrench herself free of their grasp.

"Stop resisting arrest, Jenn. You're only making matters worse for yourself," Wade warned as he brought up the rear. "Besides, crazy as shit looks, you do not have to worry about seeing the insides of a prison cell. Your crazy ass is on the way to the psych ward as soon as the psychiatric report hits my desk."

The agents put Jennifer in the backseat of an unmarked Sedan. "Where to?" the driver asked one of the agents.

"Director Stevens wants her taken straight to the interrogation unit within our building," the agent replied.

"10-4." the woman stated and drove away. At the red light, the agent turned around to get a good look at her. "Damn, Jennifer, you are a hot mess."

Jennifer raised her head off the backseat to see who it was talking to her. "Agent Soledad, you gotta let me go. I'm innocent. It was those goddam assassins who killed those people."

"Assassins?" she asked.

"Yeah, assassins. Some people call them ninjas. It was Tabitha Greene and her cousin Malice. They are all ninjas," Jennifer spoke as if confident in her words.

"You do know this conversation is being recorded?" Agent Soledad said. She turned back around shaking her head and drove through the green light.

At the federal building, Tatiana, Wade and a couple more agents stood behind the mirror tint glass of the interrogation room looking at Agent Soledad and another agent strap Jennifer down to the chair inside the all-steel interrogation cell. After Agent Soledad nodded to confirm the restraints were secure, Director Stevens sent in the on-sight Psychiatrist, who was a middle-aged, brown-skinned woman. She dismissed the agents, telling them she did not mind being alone with the patient. The agents left out and went inside the room with the others to listen in through the intercom system.

"Good morning, Jennifer. My name is Dr. Yolanda Freeman. I will be doing your mental evaluation report today. How are you feeling?"

"Let's see. My boyfriend and girlfriend were murdered on the same day. A group of my friends was murdered as well. And I'm being fucking framed for everything. I feel like shit," Jennifer replied.

Dr. Freeman typed into the iPad what she said. "So, you stated you're being framed. By whom? If you do not mind me asking."

Jennifer went into her rant about assassins, ninjas called Black Dragons and Green Mantises. How they were black and Asian only assassin's guilds from Beijing, China who had bases in New Jersey. The psychiatrist kept writing until she mentioned the name, Tabitha Greene.

"Hold on. Did you say, Tabitha Greene, as in former Special Agent Tabitha Greene?"

Jennifer nodded with a smile, thinking she might have piqued the psychiatrist's curiosity. "Yeah, that's the one. Her and her first cousin, Kenneth Freeman who they call Malice. Them and their Asian connection is behind everything."

Dr. Freeman lowered her head to keep Jennifer from seeing her expression. "Okay. So, you're saying assassins or ninjas got on a flight, flew all the way from Beijing, China to New Jersey just to make your life a living hell?"

"That's a summarized version, yes," Jennifer said.

Dr. Freeman typed a few more lines and logged out of her iPad. "Well, I think that's all the information needed to give an accurate evaluation report. Have a great day, Jennifer." She got up and left out of the cell.

The Psychiatrist stepped into the room, wherein Wade, Tatiana, Beatrice, and two more agents stood staring through the glass at Jennifer. "Anyone heard word from my nephew?" Yolanda asked.

"Wade shook his head. "No, ma'am. We are waiting to receive word from Master Malice as we speak, but I'm sure your judgment is just as valuable as is in the matter."

Yolanda logged back in the iPad and pulled up the notes she'd jot down on Jennifer. "Tarnish, retype this to fit the psych of the retarded bitch she is about to become," she said handing her the iPad. Tarnish sat down at the only table in the room and started typing.

"I'll be right back. I'm going to get the best damn needle we have in the psychiatric ward," Yolanda said and walked out. When she returned, she had the director and Agent Soledad to accompany her. They entered the room sporting serious facial expressions.

"Jennifer, it seems that you have been diagnosed as a schizophrenic. Not to mention the fact that you have previous mental issues that remain unresolved," Dr. Freeman said.

Jennifer looked up. Hearing of her past psych evaluation report shook her. "No! You do not understand! She drove me to do it. I loved her, and she cheated on me in my own damn house and Jacuzzi," Jennifer exclaimed.

"So, you're openly admitting to having anger problems and being emotionally imbalanced?" she asked while filling the needle with the medicine from the vial.

"It was not my fault! Wade help me, please!" she pleaded.

The director nodded towards the Psychiatrist. "Proceed."

Agent Soledad held Jennifer's head to the side while Yolanda injected her with the medicine. The effects kicked in immediately. Jennifer started drooling from the mouth as her words came out in a slur.

"She is all ready for the asylum," Yolanda said.

Tarnish clicked send on the report she had retyped. Afterward, she placed a call to the local asylum, informing them of the incoming report on a patient who is ready for transport. "Transport is on the way," she said as she hung up the phone.

Fifteen minutes later, two nurses walked into the interrogation cell, unstrapped Jennifer's drug-induced body from the chair, and took her away.

Willie Slaughter

Chapter Sixteen

The Freeman Estate was live. Sun had decided to throw a going-away party, which was kind of confusing to everyone since they were all getting on the flight to Beijing. Even Paul and Margaret had agreed to come along to enjoy a vacation and attend the wedding ceremonies of both Trents and their fiancés.

"To lifelong family," Sun said, raising his glass of champagne above his head. Everybody else raised theirs in salute before drinking.

"Kenny," one of the maids walked in saying. "Wade Stevens and other guests have arrived." Wade, Tatiana, Beatrice, and Yolanda walked in behind the maid.

Kenneth, Shyan, and Trent took turns hugging the fellow members of their guild. "Masters Diablo, Chalice and Tarnish, it is great seeing y'all. Especially you Aunt Yolanda," Kenneth said as he pulled her into a bear hug.

Kenneth let her go and walked to stand before his family. "Now that all the fam is here besides those who are waiting for us in Beijing, I have to get something off my chest. Life and love are two ruthless bitches when it comes to the heart."

Again, everyone raised their champagne glass in salute. They drank, ate and enjoyed each other's conversation until the call came from the pilot, saying the plane was fueled and ready to go.

Their flight landed not a second past noon. Yishi had already informed her mother that they were landing soon, so Ma Sune, Sia, Saki, and Zhia were already waiting for them at the airstrip. Before they got off the plane, Yishi wanted to address Miranda, Tabitha and her fiancé Trent.

"Before you get off this plane, there's something you need to be informed about concerning our customs. The Sune Clan doesn't react too kindly to emotions. So, do your best to keep them under control while staying on our compound," Yishi stated.

They nodded to show that they understood what Yishi was saying. But Miranda, still being curious, raised her hand, which she was quickly acknowledged by Yishi. "Yes, Miranda?"

Miranda let her hand rest on her thigh. "So, there's the Sune Clan and the Po Clan. Which clan will I be joining?" she said.

Yishi looked at Trent. "Master Trent, are you not the brother of Masters' Sun and Shyan Sune?"

Trent nodded. "In spirit, soul, and body."

"Well, Sister Miranda, you shall be Sune, which is the Green Mantis. However, we are all kindred spirits, Sune and Po. Never think differently," Yishi replied.

"What about us?" Tabitha interjected, asking.

"You two are Po," said Moon. "Now let's get off this plane, so we can get this party started." Moon was happy as ever. More so because she was back at home where her love was waiting on her.

"Like my firecracker for a granddaughter said, let's get off this plane. I'm ready for a hot bath, a fine cuisine, and the bed. We can get the party started tomorrow," Margret said. She stood up and walked towards the exit hatch. "Boy, what are you waiting on? Open this damn hatch."

Sun hurried over and opened the door. "Calm down Grandma."

"You calm down. I'm not afraid of flying, but I ain't a friend of it either." Margret said and walked on down the steps. Her husband Paul was right on her heels, carrying their bags. He squinched his eyes from the brightness of the sun.

The rest of the crew came walking down the steps with their gear slung across their shoulders inside of duffle bags. Sia and

Moon locked eyes and maintained eye contact until they met in an embrace.

"It feels so good being back in your arms," said Moon.

Sia pulled back and gave her a look. "Hopefully, you will not be running off again."

Yishi and her mother bowed to each other. It was their way of showing how much the presence of the other was missed and they were glad to see the other.

"Who do we have here?" asked Ma Sune, looking at Miranda, Trent, and Tabitha.

Yishi motioned for them to come over. "Master Ma Sune, meet Miranda, Trent, and Tabitha. Miranda, Trent and Tabitha, meet Master Ma Sune, my mother." Ma Sune bowed, and they returned the honorable greeting. "Master Ma Sune, Sister Miranda, and Master Trent shall be joining the Sune Clan."

Although Ma Sune didn't smile, nor did a facial muscle twitch, the twinkle was unmistakable in her eyes. "Hmm. We shall see to it then. Is there anything else I need to be informed of before we drive home?"

"Yes. We have two wedding ceremonies to tend to. Both, Master Trent and Miranda, as well as Trent and Tabitha, are ready to be joined in matrimony," Yishi replied.

Ma Sune nodded. "Let it be done as willed. We shall do this before other business is discussed." She noticed the questioning look in her daughter's eyes. "We have presents for you all that I know you're going to be grateful for. Let's go."

They piled in the gold, green and black Hummers that was driven by either a Golden Tiger, Green Mantis or Black Dragon. They made it to the Sune compound, where Paul, Margret, Trent, and Tabitha were shown to their sleeping quarters. They found the rooms to be to their liking. Trent showed Miranda to their room, which was the same room he had before leaving the first time.

"Your family knows how to stunt," Miranda said as she looked around the room. It was almost the same as their room was at Freeman's Estate. A mini-refrigerator, full bath, entertainment system, and a Queen size feather made bed.

"Our family, luv," Trent replied. "Let's freshen up. The noon meal will be served shortly." They unpacked and jumped in the shower, where they shared a moment of intimacy under the steaming hot water.

Sia and Moon were three rooms over doing the same thing. They kissed and rubbed their hands over the tender places on each other's body. The sighs and moans escaping from between their lips expressed the longing for each other's touch in such an intimate way. The release was so powerful that tears flowed from both Sia and Moon's eyes.

"Every second away from you seemed like hell," Moon said as she exited the shower and grabbed the drying towel. Sia stepped out and started drying herself as well.

"Tell me something I don't already know, my love?" Sia replied.

"That's an impossible task, babes," Moon said with a smirk.

Everyone had met up at the dining table for the afternoon meal. As it was the norm, no one spoke a word while eating. But as soon as the meal was over and the table cleared, Ma Sune rose to her feet, and proposed a toast.

"To our kindred spirits who have returned home and brought more of the same spirit home with them." Everyone raised their teacups in salute and agreement with her.

"We have several festivities coming up on the next sun or moon, depending on our elder's planning. There will be two weddings, and some shall embark upon their journey to rekindle the Black Dragon and Green Mantis Spirit within. I—" Ma Sune was forced to stop mid-sentence because of a Green Mantis entrance. The assassin whispered something in her right ear before leaving.

"It seems we have some hostile guests at the front gate," Ma Sune said. From the elders to the youngest stood, ready to go see what the problem was, but Ma Sune beckoned for them to return to their seats. "Please, be at peace kindred spirits. We have more than enough brothers and sisters who are in need of proving worthy of the Black Dragon and Green Mantis Spirit. Miranda, Trent and Tabitha, come with us."

Ma Sune, Zhia, Yishi, Shyan and Yuri accompanied by Miranda, Trent and Tabitha, left the dining room. Sun, Moon and their grandparents followed them out. They reached the front gate to see fifty assassins dressed in crimson red ninja suits, standing in rows of ten behind their masters. Ma Sune had to fight back a humorous smile.

"Masters Shu Lin and Phan Dao Lin, welcome," Ma Sune said. She motioned for the gates to be opened. "Enter."

Shu nor Phan replied. They walked through the opening gates, followed by their entourage of assassins. Once inside, the gates were closed, and Shu took it upon herself to address their concerns.

"Master Ma Sune, the Lin Clan feels as if we have just as much right to seize the properties you and the Po Clan have taken by force," Shu stated.

"Keywords, by force, Master Shu Lin. Would you have done such a thing?" Ma Sune replied.

"Enough of the talk," Phan Lin butted in saying. "Let's settle this according to tradition. The winner takes all, including the compound of the defeated."

Ma Sune stared Shu Lin in the eyes. "Is this what you have come here to do, Master Shu Lin? Or is this merely the babbling of your brother?"

Shu unsheathed her sword and the assassins did the same. "Master Phan Lin speaks for us all."

Ma Sune looked to her left and right. It was twelve against fifty-two. Really, ten because she would demand that Sun and Moon's grandparents return to the dining room before things got messy. "Fifty-two against ten sounds like an impossible feat to overcome. Are you sure this is what you want to do, Master Shu Lin?"

"Let master draw sword against master and student draw sword against student. We shall hold to the law of tradition, Master Ma Sune," Shu Lin stated.

Ma Sune nodded. "Understood. There's only one problem with this matter. All Sune, Po, and Yang are considered masters. For the final time, I'm asking you, Master Shu Lin, are you prepared to die?"

"No more talking, Master Ma Sune. Let the sound of steel clashing against steel and the cries of the fallen speak," Shu Lin replied.

"Very well then. Master Sun Sune instruct your grandparents to leave us," she said.

Sun didn't have to. Paul and Margret heard her loud and clear and was on their way.

Once gone, Ma Sune stretched both hands out before Shu Lin. "As you can see, neither of us are armed."

"Correction," a voice objected from behind them. It was Qi Dom Po, with Mae Za Sune and Ty Po beside him. They all carried an armful of swords. Ty Po had two short handle sickles that he handed to Moon.

"My babies," Moon said wielding the weapons expertly. "Let's get this over with."

"My thoughts exactly," Phan Lin said while initiating the attack. Out of all people, he drove straight for Ma Sune. As she pulled the sword free from the scabbard, she was already pivoting, bringing the sword around and up in a swift deadly arc. Steel met steel with a ringing, bone-jarring clang.

"Very good, Master Phan Lin," Ma Sune said.

"Taste my blade," he replied and pressed on with his attack.

Ma Sune jumped back, parrying, but Phan Lin followed. No sooner did he turn one cut than the next was upon him. The swords embraced with a deadly kiss and sprang apart only to kiss again.

Ma Sune's blood was singing within her veins. Although war was all about her, she was focused only on the opposition before her. She felt so alive knowing death balanced on every stroke. High, low, overhand, she rained down steel upon Phan Lin. Left, right, backslash, Ma Sune was swinging so hard that sparks flew when the swords came together, upswing, side slash, overhand, always counterattacking, moving counterclockwise to her opponent. Step and slide, step and strike, hacking, slashing, faster, faster, faster until the breathless Phan Lin stepped back and let the point of the sword fall to the ground. Blood drenched the front of his shirt from the cuts of the razor-sharp blade Ma Sune wielded.

"Give up and go home while you still have breath in your body, Master Phan Lin. It would be pointless killing someone who I know is no match for me or any of my kindred spirits," Ma Sune said.

Phan Lin looked around him. Almost every assassin he and his sister had accompanying them were lost, and not one of the

Sune, Po or Yang had fallen. It angered him to admit to himself how right she was, but to save his clan he did.

"Red Dragons fall back!" he commanded.

The last standing of the Lin Clan retreated. Out of the fifty-two, only thirteen remained, which included Phan and Shu.

"Master Ma Sune," Phan said while bowing. "Your reputation exceeds itself. Thank you for sparing us further humiliation."

Ma Sune waved her sword in a gesture, causing the gates to be open. "Master Phan Lin, you, your sister and clan, must learn diplomacy. Something you will not learn in the grave. Leave us be until you're ready to live with us in peace."

Phan Lin was about to respond when Shu Lin grabbed his wounded body by the shoulders and ushered him through the opened gates.

"Well, that was rude of them," Ma Sune said, watching the Red Dragons drive off. She turned her attention to Miranda, Trent, and Tabitha. "Indeed, you all are worthy of being welcomed as kindred spirits."

The three bowed silently.

"Alright, let's go wash the stench of death off. Yuri, make sure this mess is cleaned up before first moon," Ma Sune said.

"Yes ma'am," he replied and ran off towards the compound. After the gates closed, they all left from before the entrance and went to their quarters and took showers.

***

Jennifer came back to her senses and found herself locked inside a brightly lit white padded room. She wasn't in a straightjacket, which she was thankful for, but she was dressed in a paper gown. They'd stripped her of her clothes and locked her in an empty room where she couldn't do any harm to herself or others.

"Good morning. Jennifer," came a male's voice over the PA system. "I am your on-site counselor, Counselor William Fields. I will be monitoring your day by day progress. Your cooperation will tell me just how soon you'll be removed from your current solitary confinement and be placed in a more conducive environment. Do we have an understanding?"

Although the effects of the medication had worn off, Jennifer was slow at processing what the counselor stated. After replaying it several times in her mind, she nodded to state she understood.

"Great start," Counselor Fields said seeing her nod on the camera. "So, on a scale between one and ten, how do you feel today?"

"Between a three and three and a half," she replied weakly.

"Are you having suicidal thoughts?" he asked.

Everything that had happened started popping up as images within her mind. "No sir, I'm not suicidal by a long shot." Which was true. Her thoughts were homicidal, not suicidal. "Nor do I have the desire to do harm to another."

The counselor observed her body language. He typed a few notes on the iPad. "It probably will not be today, but I will see about getting you moved to population. Again, your behavior is your penalty and reward while we're waiting on the final decision. Okay?"

Jennifer nodded repeatedly. "Okay. I promise I'll be good, Counselor William Fields."

"Well, let me go see what I can do for you. I'm not making any promises. Your case is an unusual one, so let's keep our fingers crossed here," he said.

Jennifer crossed her fingers. "I'll keep them cross." Her stomach growled. "Can I please get something to eat? I'm starving."

"I bet you are due to the fact your lab results say, you're pregnant. I'll get you some food," he replied before cutting the PA system off and walking out of the security room.

Jennifer was hoping she'd heard him wrong and that the tests were faulty. But the more she thought about the way her body felt, she faced the reality of being with child. Without warning, the tears poured from her eyes like a broken dam. The father of my child is dead, Jamie is dead, and I'm locked in a mental institution for God knows how long.

'Tabitha Greene, I swear on my unborn child's life, I'm going to get out of here and fuck your world up,' she swore to herself.

A flap in the door of the room came sliding open, and a Styrofoam tray was sat in the opening. "As you ordered, Jennifer," Counselor Fields said.

She scrambled over to the flap and grabbed the first tray, thinking it was all she was getting, but as soon as she grabbed it, another one took its place. "Got to have a healthy baby."

"Thank you, Counselor William Fields," she said before the flap shut. She could hear the deadbolt being slid in place.

Jennifer sat Indian style and ate. She knew she had to get her strength up and while doing so, play by the rules. A smile splayed on her lips while she ate and plotted her escape.

'I've done it before, and I'll do it again. All for the sake of vengeance,' she thought to herself.

Chapter Seventeen

Morning came, and as Sune compound was as lively as ever. Unlike usually, everyone was going about in casual conversation. The word of the marriages between Trent and Miranda and Trent and Tabitha was all over the compound. No one cared for breakfast, they were all bustling about to get to the courtyard in a timely manner.

The combination of green, black and gold silk clothing worn by all present made for a colorful scene. Trent and his fiancé Tabitha were dressed in the Po Clan's traditional black silk long sleeve shirt and pants while the other Trent and Miranda were dressed in green. The two couples stood before the elders on the platform. Yishi, Moon, Sun, Shyan, Qi, Saki, Sia and Yuri stood about them.

Ma Sune, as straight-faced as ever, bowed before the audience. "Before we get to the most beautiful part of this rising sun, it is the tradition of Sune and Po to entertain all with the dance of the Black Dragon and Green Mantis Spirit, that this sun is righteously graced as we are graced by it and each other. It will also be an honor if Master Zhia Mi Yang will bless us with performing the dance of the Golden Tiger as well." She looked at Zhia, who nodded to consent to the proposal.

After Ma Sune was done speaking, her daughter, Yishi Pe Sune, walked off the platform by herself. Without hesitation, Yishi began the dance of the Green Mantis. Like before, she began performing the Dance of the Mantis in its calm state. She maintained the fluent and fluid movement.

Where Yishi left off Saki continued with the Dance of the Black Dragon. After she finished, Zhia Mi Yang flipped through the air effortlessly to land in the sand before the audience. Before she began, she bowed. Those who were sitting before her on the plush mats bowed back.

There was complete silence until she started performing the Dance of the Golden Tiger. Zhia Mi Yang moved with the grace and swiftness of the animal spirit. From standing katas to being on hands and knees, she performed with excellence. Her performance was so perfect that Ma Sune had to force down the smile surfacing from within.

Finally, Zhia's performance ended, but not without a standing ovation from the audience, who were following the lead of Sun and Moon's grandparents. The ceremony, although hadn't really gotten started good, was starting out awesome to the elderly couple.

"Now, we shall begin the joining of our kindred spirits in matrimony. But, before this sacred right-of-passage is performed, I must speak my peace," Mae Za Sune said. She leaned on her staff while she continued to address everyone present. "We speak of joining two souls as if they were not already one whole. Truth of the matter is, we're all one soul, moreover, we're all one spirit, mind and heart.

"We have no differences in our hearts when it comes to our kindred spirits and those whom our kindred spirits love. We will always go to the greatest lengths to protect and provide for us all as one is all, and all is one." Mae Za Sune, done speaking nodded to the high priestesses and priests, who began to move forward with the wedding ceremony.

Sun watched the ceremony in a reminiscent state, being it was performed exactly as his and Shyan's were done. Although he was enjoying seeing his brother of the guild happy, his thoughts were on the words Ty Po had spoken to him before they had gone to America.

"When you return from your journey, this rite of passage shall await you." The message was still clear within his mind. Sun didn't know exactly what journey or what would take place on it. All he knew was, he wasn't passing up the opportunity to grow wiser and sharper at being what he knew how to be.

The ceremony finally reached an ending. Ty Po walked over to stand in between the newlyweds before speaking loud enough for everyone present could hear, "Kindred spirits, Po, Sune and Yang, Black Dragon, Green Mantis, and Golden Tiger, although they have been joined in matrimony according to our culture, they must prove themselves worthy of the names given by our ancestral spirits this very moment."

Ty Po turned around to face Ma Sune and Saki Po. He bowed before saying, "Masters Ma Sune and Saki Po, come forth." They stepped forward and bowed before him. "It is time for the animal spirit within our kindred be challenged and strengthened."

Saki spoke rapidly in Mandarin. Assassins dressed in black and green ninja suits could be seen flipping on top of the flat top roofs. Everybody cleared the platform, leaving both Trents and their wives.

"Prepare for an aerial attack. It is probably the first wave assault tactic they will use," Trent said. The others responded by a nod of the head and getting in defense stances.

Ma Sune, seeing they were probably as ready as they could be, gave the signal to the Green Mantises and Black Dragons to attack. As soon as she nodded her head, the silent instruments of death descended upon the newlyweds, causing them to dive into the sand and out of the direct line of fire. The ninja stars were coming so fast they didn't have time to regain their footing. All they could do was, roll around in the sand, barely escaping death at each turn.

Being used to using ninja stars, Trent tempted fate and won. He scrambled to his feet and dove for the nearest stars laying in the sand. Without stopping his forward motion, he came up on his right knee in the kneeling position and wielded the weapon with expertise. His targets moved out of the way right before the deadly stars struck.

After Trent's show of proficiency, the assassins ceased to throw the silent projectiles in their direction. But they didn't stop their attack. Eight of the assassins surrounded the four and drew swords. Tabitha didn't give the Green Mantis standing in front of her the option to initiate the attack, she went at the assassin.

Without any weapon other than her martial arts skills, Tabitha moved swiftly to disarm and render the Green Mantis immobile. Seeing her courageous act, her husband and the others followed up with their own disarming and takedown tactics. Sia, Saki, Yishi, and Shyan looked on, admiring their strength and courage. But they knew their true test of skill was yet to come.

After the last assassin was subdued, Ma Sune called for a cease attack. "So far so good. Now, we shall move forward with this ceremony. Masters Saki, Sia, Yishi and Shyan, take-up your positions."

The four masters took their place before their opponent. Sia stood in front of Tabitha, and Saki stopped in front of Tabitha's husband. Yishi chose Trent as her opponent, which left Miranda to have to deal with Shyan.

Ma Sune nodded her head in approval of the matchups. "Here are the rules to this phase of your journey. You must successfully strike and takedown the master before you in order to end the match. The greatest feat is remaining toe to toe during this martial combat. Are you ready?"

Nobody said a word. They got in their defensive stances and stared their opponent in the eyes.

"Great, let the competition begin," Ma Sune said.

Sun took a seat next to his cousin Moon Tao Po on the front row with the other masters and elders. "How good do you think this is going to be, cuz?"

Moon shrugged her shoulders. She thought back to the day she first sparred against Sia.

Instead of engaging in formalities with Tabitha, Sia had attacked her, using pressure point strikes. Tabitha found herself unable to feel her arms, and when she tried to defend herself against another one of Sia's assaults, she realized her arms were useless.

"Tabitha, it is the Touch of the Dragon or, for your understanding, pressure point manipulation," Sia said while continuing her frontal assault. "All I'm doing is, identifying every point on your body that allows me to dominate you with little effort. A technique that will work against any size opponent."

Tabitha realized she was in no condition to defend herself or to fight back, so she did the next best thing. She evaded as best as her already aching body would allow. Sia didn't stop her attack.

"Understand the reaction to being struck in these points in order to effectively plan combinations for counters and offensive attacks. This is how you use the body's natural defense system to strike pressure points effectively," Sia instructed while administering just enough pressure so Tabitha would feel the effects.

Without warning, Sia changed her style of attack. She grabbed Tabitha's extended arm and applied pressure at the joint, causing her to wince from the pain she felt. "Another

Touch of the Dragon. But this specific touch is for joint manipulation. I'm simply using comprehension and hyperextension tactics of the joints to subdue you."

Tabitha managed to get her arm free of Sia's deadly grasp. She attempted to throw a left jab. Sia caught her fist in mid-swing, but before she could counter, Tabitha used her right to wrap Sia up in a chokehold. Sia dropped straight to the floor and used an open palm strike, hitting Tabitha at the inner right knee, causing her to stumble off balance.

"Joint manipulation can also be used to escape holds, using simple moves like this that requires no strength. Basically, ground fighting without having to wrestle." Sia said as she stood from the crouching position.

Saki watched the training in silence. She found pleasure in watching Sia teach Tabitha the way of the Black Dragon, the forward, side, circling, hooking, backward, sweeping and leaping movements. She taught her how to master the hand and foot techniques, mastering the body posture and shadow, defending the circle, trapping within the circle and cuffing through the circle.

"Tabitha, the Black Dragon Spirit is within your heart and mind. You must understand the animal within you. That way, you master the animal's movements and nature. All in all, you become the Black Dragon," Sia said.

Tired, beaten and bruised, Tabitha nodded. "Understood. And thank you for the training, Master Sia."

"Oh, it is necessary, but you are welcome. Let's continue," Sia replied.

They worked on her balance, mobility, striking power, ability to withstand stress, hands, feet, and torso coordination, intuitiveness, instinctive distancing, relaxed agile movement stimulation of self-testing energy and internal power. Although

Tabitha was getting her ass kicked, she felt herself growing stronger. 'I'll be glad when this session is over,' she thought feeling the pain Sia had administered effortlessly.

"From first-hand experience with Sia, I don't think this is going to go so well for the amateurs," Moon replied.

Sun nodded, agreeing with his cousin. They turned their attention to the matches before them. Ma Sune gave the go-ahead for the initiation to begin. As expected by Moon, Sia went at her opponent with a fierce determination to make Tabitha give her best defense.

Tabitha, remembering the rules of engagement, stood her ground, but not without sustaining injuries. From initial contact, Sia had bust her nose and lip.

"This is so unfair," Sun said.

The four masters were punishing them. Even Trent, being a master himself, wasn't being much of a match against Yishi. Every attack he tried, she countered with ease.

"Halt!" Ty Po shouted. He realized they would be enduring a lot of pain, and still wasn't guaranteed to accomplish the task of making the masters submit. "Kindred spirits, you have proven yourselves worthy of your animal spirit and to be called by the name the ancestral spirits have revealed that belongs to you."

They bowed to each other before facing the rest of the people and bowing again.

To Be Continued...
Ruthless Hearts 3
Coming Soon

Excerpts from Ruthless Hearts 4:

Blood Crazed

Jennifer, being pregnant, moved as fast as she could through the high brush surrounding the institution. Almost every ten minutes, she stopped to catch her breath and listened to make sure there weren't any dogs on her trail.

The alarm blared throughout the institution. The security guard yelled for everyone to return to their rooms for an emergency institution lockdown. One of their patients had gone missing.

"What's going?" Counselor William Fields came running down the hall still dressed in his nightclothes. He'd been called in because it was one of his clients on his caseload that went missing.

"Your favorite patient, Jennifer isn't anywhere to be found," the security guard replied.

"How? I mean, what do you mean missing?" he asked.

"Excuse my French, Counselor Fields, but the crazy woman killed another patient and covered her up in her bed to make everyone think she was sleeping. Jennifer has escaped," he answered.

William rubbed his head nervously. "Okay, okay. Put out an APB. Alert the local authorities and call Director Wade Stevens and notify his department of this mishap."

"On it, sir," the security guard replied. He stepped off to have some privacy while dialing the director's private number. The phone rung four times before there was an answer from the other end.

"I'm on the other side of the globe, right now, so whoever is calling this time of the evening, better have a damn good reason," the director said as he held the phone to his right ear. "Well?" The security guard was lost for words.

Submission Guideline

Submit the first three chapters of your completed manuscript to ldpsubmissions@gmail.com, subject line: Your book's title. The manuscript must be in a .doc file and sent as an attachment. Document should be in Times New Roman, double spaced and in size 12 font. Also, provide your synopsis and full contact information. If sending multiple submissions, they must each be in a separate email.

Have a story but no way to send it electronically? You can still submit to LDP/Ca$h Presents. Send in the first three chapters, written or typed, of your completed manuscript to:

LDP: Submissions Dept
P.O. Box 944
Stockbridge, Ga 30281

DO NOT send original manuscript. Must be a duplicate.

Provide your synopsis and a cover letter containing your full contact information.

Thanks for considering LDP and Ca$h Presents.

Coming Soon from Lock Down Publications/Ca$h Presents

BOW DOWN TO MY GANGSTA

By **Ca$h**

TORN BETWEEN TWO

By **Coffee**

THE STREETS STAINED MY SOUL **II**

By **Marcellus Allen**

BLOOD OF A BOSS **VI**

SHADOWS OF THE GAME II

By **Askari**

LOYAL TO THE GAME **IV**

By **T.J. & Jelissa**

A DOPEBOY'S PRAYER **II**

By **Eddie "Wolf" Lee**

IF LOVING YOU IS WRONG... **III**

By **Jelissa**

TRUE SAVAGE **VII**

MIDNIGHT CARTEL III

DOPE BOY MAGIC III

By **Chris Green**

BLAST FOR ME **III**

A SAVAGE DOPEBOY III

CUTTHROAT MAFIA II

By **Ghost**

A HUSTLER'S DECEIT III

KILL ZONE **II**

BAE BELONGS TO ME III

By **Aryanna**

THE COST OF LOYALTY **III**

By **Kweli**

CHAINED TO THE STREETS III

By **J-Blunt**

KING OF NEW YORK V

COKE KINGS IV

BORN HEARTLESS IV

By **T.J. Edwards**

GORILLAZ IN THE BAY V

TEARS OF A GANGSTA II

De'Kari

THE STREETS ARE CALLING II

Duquie Wilson

KINGPIN KILLAZ IV

STREET KINGS III

PAID IN BLOOD III

CARTEL KILLAZ IV

DOPE GODS II

Hood Rich

SINS OF A HUSTLA II

ASAD

TRIGGADALE III

Elijah R. Freeman

KINGZ OF THE GAME V

Playa Ray

SLAUGHTER GANG IV

RUTHLESS HEART IV

By Willie Slaughter

THE HEART OF A SAVAGE III

By Jibril Williams

FUK SHYT II

By Blakk Diamond

THE DOPEMAN'S BODYGAURD II

By Tranay Adams

TRAP GOD II

By Troublesome

YAYO III

A SHOOTER'S AMBITION III

By S. Allen

GHOST MOB

Stilloan Robinson

KINGPIN DREAMS II

By Paper Boi Rari

CREAM

By Yolanda Moore

SON OF A DOPE FIEND II

By Renta

FOREVER GANGSTA II

GLOCKS ON SATIN SHEETS II

By Adrian Dulan

LOYALTY AIN'T PROMISED II

By Keith Williams

THE PRICE YOU PAY FOR LOVE II

DOPE GIRL MAGIC II

By Destiny Skai

THE LIFE OF A HOOD STAR

By Rashia Wilson

TOE TAGZ III

By Ah'Million

CONFESSIONS OF A GANGSTA II

By Nicholas Lock

PAID IN KARMA III

By **Meesha**

I'M NOTHING WITHOUT HIS LOVE II

By Monet Dragun

CAUGHT UP IN THE LIFE II

By Robert Baptiste

NEW TO THE GAME II

By **Malik D. Rice**

Life of a Savage II

By **Romell Tukes**

Quiet Money II

By **Trai'Quan**

THE STREETS MADE ME II

By **Larry D. Wright**

<u>Available Now</u>

RESTRAINING ORDER **I & II**

By **CA$H & Coffee**

LOVE KNOWS NO BOUNDARIES **I II & III**

By **Coffee**

RAISED AS A GOON I, II, III & IV

BRED BY THE SLUMS I, II, III

BLAST FOR ME I & II

ROTTEN TO THE CORE I II III

A BRONX TALE I, II, III

DUFFEL BAG CARTEL I II III IV

HEARTLESS GOON I II III IV

A SAVAGE DOPEBOY I II

HEARTLESS GOON I II III

DRUG LORDS I II III

CUTTHROAT MAFIA

By **Ghost**

LAY IT DOWN **I & II**

LAST OF A DYING BREED

BLOOD STAINS OF A SHOTTA I & II III

By **Jamaica**

LOYAL TO THE GAME I II III

LIFE OF SIN I, II III

By **TJ & Jelissa**

BLOODY COMMAS I & II

SKI MASK CARTEL I II & III

KING OF NEW YORK I II,III IV

RISE TO POWER I II III

COKE KINGS I II III

BORN HEARTLESS I II III

By **T.J. Edwards**

IF LOVING HIM IS WRONG…I & II

LOVE ME EVEN WHEN IT HURTS I II III

By **Jelissa**

WHEN THE STREETS CLAP BACK I & II III

THE HEART OF A SAVAGE I II

By **Jibril Williams**

A DISTINGUISHED THUG STOLE MY HEART I II & III

LOVE SHOULDN'T HURT I II III IV

RENEGADE BOYS I II III IV

PAID IN KARMA I II

By **Meesha**

A GANGSTER'S CODE I &, II III

A GANGSTER'S SYN I II III

THE SAVAGE LIFE I II III

CHAINED TO THE STREETS I II

By **J-Blunt**

PUSH IT TO THE LIMIT

By **Bre' Hayes**

BLOOD OF A BOSS **I, II, III, IV, V**

SHADOWS OF THE GAME

By **Askari**

THE STREETS BLEED MURDER **I, II & III**

THE HEART OF A GANGSTA I II& III

By **Jerry Jackson**

CUM FOR ME I II III IV V

An **LDP Erotica Collaboration**

BRIDE OF A HUSTLA **I II & II**

THE FETTI GIRLS **I, II& III**

CORRUPTED BY A GANGSTA I, II III, IV

BLINDED BY HIS LOVE

THE PRICE YOU PAY FOR LOVE

DOPE GIRL MAGIC

By **Destiny Skai**

WHEN A GOOD GIRL GOES BAD

By **Adrienne**

THE COST OF LOYALTY I II

By Kweli

A GANGSTER'S REVENGE **I II III & IV**

THE BOSS MAN'S DAUGHTERS I II III IV V

A SAVAGE LOVE **I & II**

BAE BELONGS TO ME I II

A HUSTLER'S DECEIT I, II, III

WHAT BAD BITCHES DO I, II, III

SOUL OF A MONSTER I II III

Willie Slaughter

KILL ZONE
By **Aryanna**
A KINGPIN'S AMBITON
A KINGPIN'S AMBITION **II**
I MURDER FOR THE DOUGH
By **Ambitious**
TRUE SAVAGE I II III IV V VI
DOPE BOY MAGIC I, II
MIDNIGHT CARTEL I II
By **Chris Green**
A DOPEBOY'S PRAYER
By **Eddie "Wolf" Lee**
THE KING CARTEL **I, II & III**
By **Frank Gresham**
THESE NIGGAS AIN'T LOYAL **I, II & III**
By **Nikki Tee**
GANGSTA SHYT **I II &III**
By **CATO**
THE ULTIMATE BETRAYAL
By **Phoenix**
BOSS'N UP **I , II & III**
By **Royal Nicole**
I LOVE YOU TO DEATH
By Destiny J
I RIDE FOR MY HITTA
I STILL RIDE FOR MY HITTA

By **Misty Holt**

LOVE & CHASIN' PAPER

By **Qay Crockett**

TO DIE IN VAIN

SINS OF A HUSTLA

By **ASAD**

BROOKLYN HUSTLAZ

By **Boogsy Morina**

BROOKLYN ON LOCK I & II

By **Sonovia**

GANGSTA CITY

By **Teddy Duke**

A DRUG KING AND HIS DIAMOND I & II III

A DOPEMAN'S RICHES

HER MAN, MINE'S TOO I, II

CASH MONEY HO'S

By Nicole Goosby

TRAPHOUSE KING **I II & III**

KINGPIN KILLAZ I II III

STREET KINGS I II

PAID IN BLOOD **I II**

CARTEL KILLAZ I II III

DOPE GODS

By **Hood Rich**

LIPSTICK KILLAH **I, II, III**

CRIME OF PASSION I II & III

By **Mimi**

STEADY MOBBN' **I, II, III**

THE STREETS STAINED MY SOUL

By **Marcellus Allen**

WHO SHOT YA **I, II, III**

SON OF A DOPE FIEND

Renta

GORILLAZ IN THE BAY **I II III IV**

TEARS OF A GANGSTA

DE'KARI

TRIGGADALE I II

Elijah R. Freeman

GOD BLESS THE TRAPPERS I, II, III

THESE SCANDALOUS STREETS I, II, III

FEAR MY GANGSTA I, II, III

THESE STREETS DON'T LOVE NOBODY I, II

BURY ME A G I, II, III, IV, V

A GANGSTA'S EMPIRE I, II, III, IV

THE DOPEMAN'S BODYGAURD

Tranay Adams

THE STREETS ARE CALLING

Duquie Wilson

MARRIED TO A BOSS... I II III

By Destiny Skai & Chris Green

KINGZ OF THE GAME I II III IV

Playa Ray

SLAUGHTER GANG I II III

RUTHLESS HEART I II III

By Willie Slaughter

FUK SHYT

By Blakk Diamond

DON'T F#CK WITH MY HEART I II

By Linnea

ADDICTED TO THE DRAMA I II III

By Jamila

YAYO I II

A SHOOTER'S AMBITION I II

By S. Allen

TRAP GOD

By Troublesome

FOREVER GANGSTA

GLOCKS ON SATIN SHEETS

By Adrian Dulan

TOE TAGZ I II

By Ah'Million

KINGPIN DREAMS

By Paper Boi Rari

CONFESSIONS OF A GANGSTA

By Nicholas Lock

I'M NOTHING WITHOUT HIS LOVE

By Monet Dragun

CAUGHT UP IN THE LIFE

By Robert Baptiste

NEW TO THE GAME

By **Malik D. Rice**

Life of a Savage

By **Romell Tukes**

LOYALTY AIN'T PROMISED

By Keith Williams

Quiet Money

By **Trai'Quan**

THE STREETS MADE ME

By **Larry D. Wright**

BOOKS BY LDP'S CEO, CA$H

TRUST IN NO MAN

TRUST IN NO MAN 2

TRUST IN NO MAN 3

BONDED BY BLOOD

SHORTY GOT A THUG

THUGS CRY

THUGS CRY 2

THUGS CRY 3

TRUST NO BITCH

TRUST NO BITCH 2

TRUST NO BITCH 3

TIL MY CASKET DROPS

RESTRAINING ORDER

RESTRAINING ORDER 2

IN LOVE WITH A CONVICT

Coming Soon

BONDED BY BLOOD 2

BOW DOWN TO MY GANGSTA

Willie Slaughter